STARGATE
ATLÁNTIS ™

FROM THE DEPTHS

AMY GRISWOLD

FANDEMONIUM BOOKS

An original publication of Fandemonium Ltd, produced under license from MGM Consumer Products.

Fandemonium Books
United Kingdom
Visit our website: www.stargatenovels.com

S T A R G A T E
A T L A N T I S ™

METRO-GOLDWYN-MAYER Presents
STARGATE ATLANTIS™
JOE FLANIGAN RACHEL LUTTRELL JASON MOMOA JEWEL STAITE
ROBERT PICARDO and DAVID HEWLETT as Dr. McKay
Executive Producers BRAD WRIGHT & ROBERT C. COOPER
Created by BRAD WRIGHT & ROBERT C. COOPER

WWW.MGM.COM

Print ISBN: 978-1-905586-81-3 Ebook ISBN: 978-1-80070-064-2

CHAPTER ONE

ELIZABETH WEIR unpacked the last of the pieces of pottery, placed it on the office shelf, and considered the effect. Through the window, a gray light filtered in from the chilly pier outside. It was summer in Atlantis's new home, but that meant only more cold rain than snow, and she missed the sunlit seas of their first home in the Pegasus Galaxy. The city of Atlantis hadn't changed since she left, but so much else about life in the city had.

"Settling in?" John Sheppard asked, leaning against the doorframe and regarding her efforts at interior decorating.

Case in point, one Colonel Sheppard, now the acting commander of the Atlantis expedition. The first week after they'd arrived in the Pegasus Galaxy, she would have given even odds that he'd wind up court-martialed. The first year after they'd arrived in the Pegasus Galaxy, she would have given even odds that he'd wind up dead. But now he was still here, a steady presence after years with the expedition while she had died, Ascended, and returned.

"I thought I might as well get comfortable," she said. "I'm still hoping to go back to Earth soon, but as long as I'm in limbo here…"

"…you need an office," John said. He shifted awkwardly. "You know that you could have your old office back."

"That's the Atlantis commander's office," Elizabeth said. "And since I'm not the Atlantis commander and you are…"

"For the moment." How long the IOA would take to name a new commander for the Atlantis expedition was as unanswerable a question as when they would pronounce themselves satisfied that Elizabeth was human, free of Replicator programming, and cleared to return to Earth. Elizabeth wasn't certain that John would escape being named the next commander, and wasn't entirely certain that he wanted to escape the responsibility, despite his protestations.

It was strange not be certain. Every day brought reminders that she'd missed three long years in the lives of the people she had once called her closest friends.

She shook her head briskly, reminding herself how fortunate she was. "I appreciate the SGC sending these boxes out to me, although it's a little odd: since most of my personal effects were sent back to my family, all that was left in storage were things from Pegasus that weren't cleared to be released. So I have this, from P2J-4215 —" She held up a sculpted serpentine figure carved from a mineral not naturally occurring on Earth. "But not my coffee mugs."

"I could round some up for you."

"Thank you, but I think I'm up to tackling that challenge myself."

"They still haven't notified your family?"

"I asked Mr. Woolsey to wait until I was cleared," Elizabeth said. "As long as there's any doubt that I'm human —"

"Which there isn't."

"Or any possibility that my return will be significantly delayed," she went on, and John frowned, clearly unable to argue that the IOA was always efficient and prompt. "I can't put my mother through that. I'll send her a message when I'm on my way home." She set down the pottery snake and settled into a chair that she couldn't help noticing was less comfortable than her old one. "So, what have we got on the schedule today?"

"Not the Wraith, not the Vanir, and not the Genii. For a change."

"Do we ever actually schedule the Wraith?" Elizabeth asked dryly.

"These days it happens. My big excitement of the morning is meeting with the biologists who want to talk about…" He consulted his tablet. "'Genetic anomalies in the local sea life.' I'm guessing they want me to authorize more exploratory jumper missions to the ocean floor, which given that we're not under attack this week I may actually be able to do."

"You mean we could actually do some research on the Pegasus Galaxy?"

"I think we still do that. Want to sit in?"

It wasn't really her area of expertise — she'd always focused on the cultural aspects of the mission, and her oversight of the science team had largely been to direct their efforts to resolve one crisis after another. Still, she couldn't say she had anything more pressing to do, and she appreciated the effort to include her.

"Why not," she said. "Just let me stop by the mess hall and pick up a regulation coffee mug."

***

The marine biology lab was damp and cold, the cold-water tanks seeming on the verge of icing over and the heated tanks sending up steam that dripped down the wall behind them. Dr. Moore seemed perfectly comfortable in his shirtsleeves, although John couldn't help noting that several of the research assistants were wearing fingerless gloves and had layered turtlenecks under their uniform jackets.

"This has been a tremendous opportunity for us," Dr. Moore said, leading them around tanks to the display screen on one wall. Fish milled around the nearest tank in a silvery school. "We finally have the chance to study a cold-water ocean ecosystem in the Pegasus galaxy at length without having to mount an expedition through the gate."

"Fine for you," one of the research assistants said, rubbing her hands together. "That's what you're interested in. My dissertation research was on tropical reefs."

"There are some unusual reefs on M7J-44X3," Moore offered, the light from the tanks throwing blue shadows across his face. One of the few science specialists from the original Atlantis mission who hadn't either died or returned to a more normal life on Earth, his close-shaved hair was beginning to gray, but he retained his enthusiasm for icy oceans.

"Through the gate," the assistant muttered.

"What have we got?" Elizabeth said, and then shot

John an apologetic look. "I'm sorry, that's your line."

He shook his head to show no apology was needed. "What *have* we got?"

"We've been working with the genetics team to do some gene sequencing on the samples we've taken so far," Dr. Moore said. "Most of the results were interesting but not particularly surprising. We're mapping out the relationships between various species in a number of local ecosystems."

"But…" John prompted. In his experience in Atlantis, this was the point at which someone usually said "but we found out that the water is inhabited by jellyfish that suck out people's life force," or "but we discovered that some of the fish are actually robot spies for an alien threat we haven't even got on our radar yet."

"But one of them stands out in complete contrast to the rest. The giant squid — or, actually, they may be more closely related to colossal squid — you've observed them near Atlantis?"

"I think everyone's seen them," John said. The creatures were apparently curious, and tentacles had been observed snaking out of the water to snatch unsecured gear, unguarded lunches, and on one memorable occasion, Jack O'Neill's fishing pole.

Dr. Moore brought up video footage on the display screen. Underwater, the creatures made an impressive display, brilliant patterns of color dancing across their skins, shifting and changing as they moved. "They're an apex predator, and one of the few large aquatic predators we've seen since we arrived. We suspect that if there were native large predatory species, the squid hunted them to extinction shortly after... as we hypothesize... the squid were introduced."

"You think they're not native to this planet," Elizabeth said.

"Almost certainly not. Their genetic makeup is radically different in significant ways from the native species on this world, and we've found no species that could possibly be close relatives. There are general similarities to squid on Earth, but those are the types of similarities we see on all the planets where the Ancients seeded life. Wherever this species evolved into its present form, I don't think it was here."

"So how did they get here?" John asked. "This planet didn't have a Stargate until we got here."

"It might have been accidental," Elizabeth said. "A ship fills water tanks on one world, expels wastes on another... invasive species have been transmitted that way on Earth."

"You'd think they'd notice a ten-meter squid."

"It's certainly possible that they were transported here accidentally, perhaps in a juvenile form, or as fertilized eggs that had been deposited in water being transported," Dr. Moore said. "However, there is another possibility that's a little troubling."

"We're listening," John said.

"We know this was one of the planets where the Ancient scientist Janus experimented with humans and Iratus bugs and ended up creating the Wraith," Dr. Moore said. "He transported the Iratus bugs here in order to do that. Finding another type of non-native life on this planet does raise the question of whether there might be some connection."

"You think Janus might have been trying to combine humans and squid?" John wished he could rule that out as something that no one could possibly have wanted, not even the Ancients, but he had learned not to put a whole lot past them. Personally he wasn't a fan of things with tentacles, except in fried and crunchy form.

"I couldn't begin to speculate what he might have wanted to do, except... cephalopods on Earth are remarkably intelligent, but constrained by their relatively short lifespans. Most live only a few years, and many species die immediately after mating. We know that one of the things Janus wanted to achieve from his experiments was to prevent humans from aging. Working with squid might have provided an interesting way to test whatever mechanism he intended to use."

"So, you think he might have been trying to combine the squid and the Iratus bugs." That didn't sound better. In fact, it sounded significantly worse.

"I think it's possible the squid were originally brought here as subjects for Janus's experiments. I won't commit myself more than that. But if that's the case, it increases the importance of closely observing the creatures and their behavior."

"So that we can find out if we're sharing the planet with life-sucking Wraith squid," John said.

"We probably aren't," Dr. Moore said. "At least, there's no definite evidence to suggest that we are."

"Even so," Elizabeth said. "Let's find out." She looked sideways at John. "If we have the resources to proceed with this research project."

That wasn't exactly asking him for permission, but it still felt weird to have Elizabeth asking him for permission in the first place, so he figured it would do. "We do right now. Better make the most of it. If Janus had anything to do with this, we need to find out what he was up to."

"His experiments did tend to have an amazing potential to go wrong," Elizabeth said.

"And you'd think that messing around with people's DNA trying to turn them into super-beings would work so well," John said dryly.

"As a former 'super-being'… not so much."

John shrugged rather than replying, because he thought they'd come to some kind of unspoken agreement not to talk about the time she'd spent first frozen in space and then on another plane of existence as an Ascended being. You had to take that kind of thing in stride in Atlantis, but that didn't mean you entirely got used to it.

"Pack your gear," Dr. Moore said to his glum-looking assistant. "And let's go look for some squid."

***

Evan Lorne had imagined a lot of futures for himself when he joined the Air Force, but submarine pilot hadn't been one of them. As he steered the jumper through the crystal blue water a few meters beneath the surface, he wondered whether it might be worth looking for some Navy personnel with the ATA gene. It would have been nice to be able to hand over squid-searching duty to someone who could honestly say that oceanography was their specialty.

"All right, doc," he said. "I'm reading some large life signs about 500 meters ahead. I'm going to bring us in closer."

"Try not to disturb them," Dr. Moore said.

"I'll do my best," Lorne said, although exactly how to bring the jumper in closer without disturbing whatever marine life was out there seemed like a good question. While the shield was engaged to turn the jumper into a submersible craft, it wasn't possible to hide behind a cloak, as convenient as that might have been. He settled for advancing at a steady speed, while Moore and his assistant, Tatiana Ivanova, crowded forward to peer out the forward window in search of any sign of giant squid.

The first sign that they were on the right track was a flash of moving color in the distance. Lorne had seen the giant squid nosing around Atlantis, and had learned to classify them as harmless, if alarming when they appeared unexpectedly while he was trying to make sure the underwater parts of Atlantis were staying free of ice. The flash of color was followed by another, and then another, lighting up the grey water.

"Are those what we're looking for?" Lorne asked.

Moore leaned forward excitedly. "I think so. How many are you picking up?"

Lorne whistled. "A lot." He could see the water swirling with them now, their bodies flashing a rainbow of colors in intricate patterns. "Are they actually glowing?"

"I think there's an electrical effect enhancing their luminescence," Dr. Moore said. "It would make their optical signals easier to detect, and it might also have the effect of warning away enemies or attracting prey."

"These thing can't zap us, though, like an electric eel?"

"That would be interesting," Moore said, which didn't really seem to answer Lorne's question. "But, no, we've seen nothing to suggest that directly," he continued, possibly in answer to Lorne's expression. "Certainly their beaks seem well-adapted for hunting, and as apex predators, they have limited need for defense, unless it's against other members of their species. Which is possible, of course. They may compete to mate, or over access to scarce resources... but we're behind the jumper's shields, in any event."

"Which sounds like it's probably a good thing," Lorne said.

"How many of the creatures are you reading?"

"A hundred, maybe? This thing's just picking up life signs and approximate size, though. If they're gathering around a source of food, some of these blips on the life sign detector might be their prey, if their prey is also pretty large."

"Mmm," Moore said noncommittally. "This could be feeding behavior, of course, that's a possibility. What do you think, Ivanova?"

It was the same tone that Lorne's instructors at the Academy had used to say things like "is that your answer?", which generally meant "that's the wrong answer."

"That's a lot of signaling for feeding behavior," Ivanova said. "Look at those patterns pop."

"I see it, I see it. I trust that we're recording this?"

"Sure," Lorne said, and checked that the jumper's sensors were recording the riot of colors and patterns flashing through the water in front of them. The squid were moving in complex patterns, forming into little knots and then separating, some darting from group to group. On their sides, colorful patterns flashed in luminescent blues and reds, darkening to greyscale stripes and brightening to bold splotches that made them look like they'd been finger-painted by a little kid.

"Squid on Earth aren't social hunters," Moore said. "And if this were coordinated hunting behavior, I'd expect to see them driving a shoal of fish or some other prey in particular directions."

"Aggressive behavior?" Ivanova suggested. "They could be competing for food."

"So where's the prey?" Moore squinted at the life sign readings now overlaid on the viewscreen in front of them. "There's nothing here that looks like fish attempting to escape a predator. If they were feeding on something less mobile, like jellyfish, I'd expect to see them moving in, snatching food, perhaps displaying aggressive signals toward nearby individuals. This…"

"Could be mating behavior," Ivanova said.

"I don't think so. It's too complex. Keep recording."

"I promise, I'm recording."

"I'm seeing repeating patterns," Ivanova said. "See that, red shifting to blue, like an arrow, always oriented in the same direction —"

"Migration behavior? We could be watching a migratory group form —"

"There are other repeating patterns, with variations. We're looking at something at least as complex as birdsong here. At least."

Both scientists were squeezing forward, their noses nearly up against the viewscreen. Lorne found himself craning forward to see, too, despite knowing essentially nothing about the biology of squid. One thing he'd discovered while ferrying scientists all over the Pegasus Galaxy was that enthusiasm for any subject, no matter how mind-numbingly boring on the face of it — plants, rocks, watching old ruins get older — tended to be contagious.

"Humor me for a moment," Moore said, leaning back in his seat and squinting at the squid as they darted back and forth through the water, surprisingly swift for creatures their size. "Is it possible to run the footage we're getting of their communication through the jumper's computer and see if it suggests meaningful groupings of symbols?"

"You think it's some kind of language?"

Moore shrugged. "The patterns we're seeing are suggestive. So —"

"That's not something that the jumper's computers are set up to do," Lorne said. "We can take this back and let one of the linguists take a look at it. This might be right up Lynn's alley." William Lynn had come out to Atlantis the year before as a civilian linguist, and while his specialty was analyzing the origins of the Wraith language in the language of the Ancients, Lorne thought he might be willing to take a break to figure out whether the squid were talking.

"Let's get some more recordings," Moore said. "Can you get us in closer?"

As Lorne edged the jumper cautiously closer, the

squid veered out of his way. Many of them were longer than the jumper, and he tried to give them a wide
berth. While they hadn't proven aggressive so far, he
wasn't sure he liked the idea of being swarmed by them.
Near him, the creatures' flashing colors changed their
pattern even more rapidly, and groups of the creatures
circulated in tight knots before zooming off to other
parts of the large shoal. The tentacles and arms trailing
through the water gave the appearance of enormous,
writhing knots of seaweed, or possibly something out
of an old monster movie.

"I think we're upsetting them," Lorne said.

"Can't you use the cloak?"

"Not without dropping the shield, and unless you
want to risk having to swim home, we're not going to
do that." He backed the jumper away, still recording.
"We're going to have to surface soon," he said. "Using
the shield underwater eats power. In fact, it's dropping
pretty fast." He frowned at the readings. "Actually, a
lot faster than it's supposed to. I think we'd better take
this jumper back and get it checked over."

"It would be ideal if we could bring one of the creatures back with us," Moore said.

"Considering their size, how are we actually going to
do that?" Lorne asked, hoping he sounded more patient
than he felt. He'd learned to expect the scientists to say
things like "maybe we could bring the glowing tree back
to the botany lab" and "it looks like it may have poi-
sonous fangs, let's get a closer look!" and "it's possible
that the radiation it's emitting is some kind of greet-
ing, so if we put on radiation suits, maybe we can say a

proper hello." He'd also learned that it was important to introduce practical considerations early and often if they were actually going to be heard.

"They're not going to fit in a bait cooler," Ivanova said. "We might be able to snag another tissue sample if someone goes out there in a wet suit." She sounded wearily sure of who that someone was likely to be.

"Let's go talk to the linguists first," Lorne said. "I don't like the idea of staying out here in a malfunctioning jumper, and if there's any chance that we're dealing with an intelligent species here, scraping off samples of their skin isn't a great way to say hello."

He brought the jumper around, heading back toward Atlantis, and then frowned as the life sign readings changed. "It looks like we've attracted some attention."

"They're pursuing?" Moore asked. "Possibly trying to drive us out of their territory, don't you think?" The last was presumably to Ivanova, who shrugged. "In that case, they shouldn't pursue us for long."

"Let's put some distance between us and our friends, just to be sure," Lorne said. He surfaced, the jumper shedding water as it lifted into the air, and then checked the life sign readings again. "Ah — doc, they still seem to be following us."

"Ridiculous," Moore said. "They certainly can't see us now that we've left the water."

Lorne tested this comforting theory by setting a zig-zag course back toward Atlantis. While the squid didn't follow his zigs and zags, and quickly lagged behind the jumper's airspeed, they did maintain their own steady course in the direction of the city. And not just a few angry squid — it looked like the whole group of the creatures was heading directly for Atlantis.

"It could be a coincidence," Ivanova offered, leaning over his shoulder to see the life-sign readouts. "Maybe they're done with whatever they were doing, and now they're ready to move on."

On a hunch, Lorne had been expanding the radius of his life-sign scan, and he brought the readings up on the heads-up display. "I'm not sure how that explains this."

Around the city, from every direction, life-sign readings were arrowing toward Atlantis.

"It looks like we're going to have a whole lot of company," he said.

CHAPTER TWO

"AND ALL these life sign readings are squid?" Elizabeth asked. Across the conference room table, John looked at Ronon, who shrugged as if to say that this wasn't a problem they ever had on Sateda. Teyla looked concerned, while from the way that Rodney had his head bent over his tablet she wasn't certain he was paying attention. William Lynn, the linguist, had his tablet propped on the table in front of him like a student anxious for a chance to read his notes in class.

"It looks like it," Lorne said on the radio. "They're pretty speedy, too. If they keep moving at this speed, the first of them are going to reach the city in about an hour."

"Raise the shields," Elizabeth said. There was a pause, and John cleared his throat. "I'm sorry. Colonel Sheppard?"

"Raise the shields," John said. "Not that we're probably in that much danger from angry squid."

"If something hits the underwater observation windows hard enough, it could be a problem," Lorne said. "We could have some flooding of the lower levels and some damage that would be a pain to repair. And there are critical systems on the underside of the city; they're not fragile, exactly, but it wouldn't do them any good to have a giant squid grab them and try to twist them apart."

"So let's avoid that," John said.

"Not exactly a city-wide crisis, though," Rodney said. "Unless we plan to make a lot of calamari, I'm not sure why we need a full briefing on this. Keep the shield up until they finish mating, or feeding, or whatever it is they're doing —"

"There is still the possibility that the squid represent an experiment similar to the one that created the Wraith," Teyla said.

"Yes, but do we have the slightest bit of evidence that they do?"

Lynn shifted in his seat, and John turned his way. John used fewer words in his moderation of the conversation around the table than Elizabeth would have, but Lynn seemed clear enough that he had the floor. "We don't," Lynn said. "But —" He spoke up over Rodney's attempt to launch into a dismissal of the entire topic of the squishy sciences. "But, that said," he went on with determination, "there are some indications we may be dealing with an intelligent species."

"Which are?" John prompted.

"I've taken a quick look at the data that Moore and Ivanova brought back. I should prefer to have several days to analyze them and report my findings, rather than an hour —"

"Try doing nuclear physics in ten minutes while in constant danger of dying," Rodney muttered.

"But I've arrived at some tentative preliminary conclusions, granting that this is a highly inadequate sample —"

"No one is asking you for data that will survive peer review," Elizabeth said. "What are you seeing?"

"There are color variations that occur in complex patterns with partial repetition," Lynn said. "At first I wondered if we were looking at something like birdsong — very complex learned behavior, and certainly a primitive form of communication, but not symbolic language. But something about the patterns was nagging at me, so I ran the whole thing through the city's computers, looking for any relevant data, and what I found was this." He turned his tablet around to display a rapidly changing series of colors and patterns.

"The Ancients were interested in squid?" Ronon asked.

Lynn looked pleased, like a teacher whose student had provided the correct next line to carry the lecture forward. "Not from anything I've found. But they did record this visual code, a form of the Ancient language that could be conveyed entirely through color and pattern. I'm not sure whether the Ancients created it themselves — frankly, I'm not sure why they would have needed to — or whether it was created by some group of humans in the Pegasus galaxy. If you didn't have the technology for subspace communication…"

"You could use this to signal between spaceships," Rodney said, finally looking grudgingly interested. "I see that."

"Or aircraft," John said. "Or submarines. Okay. Is this what the squid are using?"

Lynn's eyes slid sideways. "Well. That's where it becomes relevant that we have an extremely small sample of extremely complex communication that has almost certainly evolved significantly from this system, even if it was based on it originally."

"Dr. Lynn…" Elizabeth began.

"Yes or no," John said.

"A definite maybe. I've identified several different groupings that look like they could represent words. Some of them make more sense than others, I'm afraid."

"So you're not sure," Rodney said. "Personally, I'm leaning toward no."

"You sound skeptical," Teyla said. "We have seen stranger things."

"Sure, but it's the time frame," Rodney said. "Even if the ancestors of these squid were smart enough to talk and learned how to do it from the Ancients, would their descendants really remember enough Ancient to still be using it thousands of years after the Ancients left?"

"Human worlds do," Ronon said.

"Yes, but most human worlds have contact with other human worlds," Lynn said. "Contact through the Stargate helps to prevent linguistic drift. Most other worlds that have been isolated for a very long time have had written language for at least part of that time, which is another stabilizing factor. The squid, presumably, have neither."

"Which side of this are you arguing?" John asked.

"I told you, I don't have enough data. And we're not going to get it with the shields up. Why don't we leave the shields down until we have a chance to try to establish communication?"

"That's an option," Elizabeth said, but John shook his head.

"Let's see what they do when they get here," he said. "If they're just passing through, we can lower the shield once they've moved on. But I don't think we want to test the structural integrity of the docking bay doors or the observation windows by letting them get pounded on by angry squid."

***

"There's something very odd about these shield fluctuations," Zelenka said.

Lorne frowned and stretched to look over his shoulder, although he couldn't make much of the readouts scrolling across Zelenka's screen. He understood the jumper's controls from a pilot's point of view, but he couldn't tell much from the readout except that the jumper's power had been dropping. "Think the shield generator's giving out?"

"If so, I am at a loss to explain why. And it has been performing perfectly in every test I've put it through so far." Zelenka tapped his fingers on the tablet. "It could simply be a result of operating the jumper underwater," he said. "That does drain shield power quickly, but the rate should be directly proportional to the depth that the jumper is submerged, because it's a function of the pressure being exerted on the jumper by the water. But look at these graphs, here. The power is declining as expected, and then — bang, it begins plunging. Then the drain on the power decreases, even though the jumper appears to be remaining at a constant depth."

"So what's wrong with it?"

"It's possible that the depth sensors are malfunctioning. If you drifted deeper, that might explain the increased power consumption."

"I don't think so," Lorne said. "That was at the point

that we were observing the squid, and they were pretty near the surface, doing whatever they were doing. Part of this time, the jumper wasn't moving at all. I think I would have noticed if we'd actually been sinking."

"While you were observing the squid?" Zelenka said, looking up sharply from the tablet.

"Yeah. And the power drain stopped when we moved away from them. But I can't think of any reason why being near them would affect a shield generator."

"Let us go and talk to the biologists," Zelenka said. "This is sounding more like a biological sciences problem."

"Is that a good thing, or a bad thing?"

"Bad, as far as I am concerned. Physics is easier."

They found Dr. Moore and Dr. Lynn in the marine biology lab. "We're missing a channel of communication," Lynn said. "These symbols are clearly intelligently used, but they're incomplete. If there's a perceptible electrical field —" He broke off as he caught sight of Lorne and Zelenka. "I'm sorry, does Sheppard want this yesterday? Because I think he's going to have to settle for tomorrow."

"No, this is idle curiosity, crossed with not-so-idle worry," Zelenka said. "Tell me, is there anything about the biology of the squid that suggests that they might be able to produce interference with the jumper's shield generator?"

"Interesting," Moore said. Zelenka winced.

"I'm going to take that as a 'yes,'" Lorne said.

"The squid are producing electrical signals of some kind, and we think that may be part of their communication method," Dr. Moore said. "While it's unlikely that such a signal could interfere with the jumper's shield generator, it does become less unlikely if you have a reason to ask that question."

Zelenka muttered something unhappy-sounding in Czech. "I think you should take the jumper back out and see if you can reproduce the phenomenon."

"Even if the squid do interfere with the jumper's shields, we should be able to steer clear of them in future," Lorne said. "It's a problem, but maybe not a big problem."

Zelenka threw up his hands. "There are thousands of these creatures converging on the city. The city that is protected by a larger version of the same shield generator, yes? So what do we think is going to happen when we are surrounded by the squid?"

"Okay, that's a big problem."

"Please go and get me more data."

"Will do," Lorne said.

From the air, Atlantis at night was beautiful as always, its strong geometric lines jutting up toward the sky like illuminated shafts of ice. The shield was a marbleized bubble above him and, once it had closed behind him, the city looked like it was under a dome of antique glass. Above the dark sea, the aurora shimmered on the horizon, sheets of wavering green and blue streaking the sky.

Below, around the city, a tentacle broke the water, and then another. The water rippled in currents that didn't seem natural. He put a cautious amount of distance between the jumper and the squid before submerging and looking for a smaller grouping to approach.

He returned with news he knew the scientists weren't going to like. "Every time I get near the squid, my shield power starts dropping," he said. "The effect is clearly stronger the more of the creatures are around, so if you plot the declines in shield power against the life-sign readings —"

"It's possible that we could get some information about how the creatures are using their electrical generation to communicate," Dr. Moore said.

"Yes, true, but I think Major Lorne's point was that we could use the life-sign readings to get some idea of how much shield power declines as more creatures enter the area," William said.

"That would be a good idea, yes," Zelenka said. "We need to find out —" He was interrupted by his radio activating. "Yes, Zelenka here."

"Dr. Zelenka, this is Airman Salawi up in the control room. We're reading some power fluctuations in the city's shield — it's not a problem with the ZPM power, or if it is, it's not showing up on the main board, but the shield generator itself doesn't seem to be working at full efficiency."

"It seems that we have more data," Zelenka said, pushing his glasses up his nose. "I will go see what we can do to keep our shields functioning, and you can wake up Colonel Sheppard and explain the problem."

"And you know I just love to do that," Lorne said dryly.

***

A few hours later, as the sun rose over the icy sea, John nursed a cup of coffee in the conference room where he'd called an early morning meeting and wished that he was having a squid-free day. "They aren't showing any signs of leaving?"

"That would be nice," Rodney said. "But, no. We still have a squid convention surrounding the city, and they're definitely interfering with the city's shields. Right now they're functioning at about 25 percent of their normal strength. That means the squid themselves can't get through, but if anyone shows up with energy weapons, we're going to be sitting ducks."

"Right now. You think it's going to get worse?"

"There are more of the things still arriving, and we're picking up life signs as far out in the ocean as we can detect them, all converging on the city. Unless something changes, we're going to reach a critical mass of squid that's going to overwhelm the shield generators completely. At that point, these things will be free to tear up the underside of the city, and there's a lot for them to wreck down there. With all the trouble we had keeping essential components free of ice, this is going to be worse."

"Is there anything you can do to keep the shields working?" John asked.

Rodney shrugged. "We might be able to reconfigure them, but it's going to take us some time."

"If it is possible," Radek said.

"It's probably possible. But that still leaves us vulnerable in the short term, and I can't guarantee that any major reconfiguration won't be more of a drain on our ZPM than keeping the shields up like this is already. There are reasons we don't usually keep the city shielded all the time."

"Dr. Moore says that the limited supply of food in the area will pose a problem for the squid if they attempt to remain near the city in these numbers," Teyla said. "There are not enough fish near the city to support this many large predators for long."

"Which makes sense given that we haven't seen groupings like this before," Elizabeth said. "We have to assume that the small population of squid we normally see near the city represents the number that can live here on anything like a permanent basis."

"So they'll leave when they run out of food, right?" Ronon said, leaning back in one of John's office chairs. "If they're an intelligent species, that's the smart thing to do."

"I still don't have enough data to be certain how they will behave," Lynn said from the other chair.

"Scientists always say that," Ronon said.

"Yes, that's science." The debate between the two seemed good-natured; they'd become friends since they began working together in the field, especially as Lynn was genuinely interested in what Ronon could tell him about the Satedan writing system and culture, and Ronon seemed more willing than he once had been to talk about his home planet. It probably helped that it wasn't entirely a burned-out wreck anymore.

"If there's any chance that they are an intelligent species, we need to find that out and find some way to communicate with them and ask them to leave," Elizabeth said. "If they're not an intelligent species, and something about Atlantis is attracting them to converge in this area, we need to find out so that we can stop doing it. We need our shields back, and I also don't want to be responsible for the extinction of an entire species of marine life, intelligent or not."

"We've been here for almost two years," John said. "We've never had this problem before."

She shrugged. "Then something's changed. We should figure out what."

"We could move the city," Rodney said.

John looked at him sideways. "And yet you don't seem enthusiastic about that."

"It would use a lot of power and introduce a whole new set of risks. This isn't a passenger plane we're talking about. It's an entire city that was never designed to maneuver in atmosphere. Every time we've had to land it, we've ended up damaging something." Rodney shrugged. "We can do it if we have to, but I'd rather not have to."

"And whatever is attracting the creatures to the city may lead them to follow us to a new location," Teyla said.

"Can't we drive these things away from the city?" Ronon asked.

"We could stun them," John said. "But we're talking about moving a couple of thousand squid. We can't exactly stuff them all in the backs of jumpers."

"Dr. Moore recommended specifically against stunning them unless we don't mind it being potentially fatal," Lynn said. "He thinks that because they use electrical energy to communicate, stunning them is likely to disrupt that activity. At best, we'd render them unable to communicate, either temporarily or permanently. At worst, we might well kill them."

"Which would at least get us our shields back," Rodney said. "But if we're assuming that's unacceptable, then I have more bad news, which is that any modulations we make to the shields to prevent the squid's electrical energy from interfering with them are likely to have similar effects. Depending on what we have to do to keep the shields up, we may actually be creating a giant bug zapper surrounding the entire city. Unless we can somehow communicate 'very dangerous, don't touch,' we're going to wind up with fried squid."

"That's a lot of calamari," John said. "And these are intelligent beings who just happen to look like a seafood special. We're not going to go there. So, okay, we can't move them and we may not be able to fix the shields until we can talk to them. What can we do?"

"Work on talking to them," Elizabeth said. "Let me go out in a jumper and see if I can establish contact with them. The best solution we have to all our problems is to get them to agree to move away from the city voluntarily."

"I should go as well," Lynn said immediately. "If we modify the jumper's cloak to project color and pattern, we may be able to establish two-way communication. From what Dr. Zelenka says, that's theoretically possible — the cloak already produces some visible light as a byproduct of its functioning, so it's just a matter of altering its intensity and wavelength. If I can get enough data, and run it through the Stargate translation program, we could be able to speak to these creatures and find out why they're here."

"You want to go out in a jumper and take it underwater where there are literally thousands of squid, and you want to modify the cloaking device so that the jumper can't be cloaked or shielded," John said. "Assuming McKay and Zelenka can get that to work."

"Sure, let's also put wheels on it so that you can drive it on the highway," Rodney said. "Do you realize that we're going to have to... yes, all right, fine, we can probably do it."

"Quickly," John said.

"Like everything else around here, yes."

"Great. I'm still not convinced this is a good idea." He hated having to be the voice of reason; he was much more comfortable throwing out the wild ideas and letting someone more cautious shoot down the ones that really weren't good plans. But someone had to be the voice of reason, and from the look in Elizabeth's eye, it wasn't going to be her today.

"We can hardly talk to the squid if we're hiding from them, so we wouldn't want the cloak anyway," Elizabeth said. "And considering what their electromagnetic field is doing to the city's shield, we probably can't count on either one being effective in their presence."

"Which is my point."

"So we wait for Dr. Zelenka and Dr. McKay to modify the jumper's cloak, which will also give Dr. Lynn more time to work on his translations, and then we go talk. We're going to have to trust that we can either establish peaceful communication or get out of the way quickly if that doesn't seem to be an option."

John opened his mouth to say "all right, but you

can't go," and then shut it again. He wasn't certain he had a good reason, besides the chill that went up his spine at the idea of Elizabeth putting herself into danger again. They'd only just gotten her back. That wasn't something he'd ever expected. He knew better than to expect it to happen twice.

"Fine. But I'm flying the jumper," he said.

Elizabeth gave him a look. "You've just finished explaining how dangerous this is. You know that's exactly why the commander of the Atlantis expedition shouldn't be the one to go, right?"

"You know that's the worst part of this job, right?" John replied.

"And here I thought you'd think it was the paperwork."

"Take Teyla with you, and Lorne can fly the jumper."

"Thank you, Colonel." She smiled a little. "You know, I might come to enjoy being on the other side of that desk."

"You know I'm not assigning you to a gate team, right?" He wasn't sure she was really at a point in her life to take up sprinting for the Stargate as an occupation.

"I'm a diplomat," Elizabeth said, sobering. "If I'm not here to talk to people in difficult situations, I'm not sure why I am here."

"All right," John said, repressing his misgivings. "Go talk to the squid."

CHAPTER THREE

THE JUMPER cut through the dim water, the hum of its engines far quieter than the mechanical groaning of any Earth submarine Elizabeth had ever visited. It only drove home the fact that it wasn't at all designed for the use they were currently putting it to. Elizabeth comforted herself with the thought that they weren't descending to depths where they'd be in immediate danger if the jumper sprung a leak.

Around the undercarriage of Atlantis, the shield shimmered, and dark tentacled forms moved in front of it. Lorne gave them a wide berth, bringing the jumper to a point where they could see the creatures but weren't in the midst of them. Immediately, several of the large cephalopods turned and approached the jumper, not touching it, but circling it in the water, tentacles and wider, flattened arms trailing behind them.

"All right, Dr. Lynn," Elizabeth said. "Your advice?"

Lynn looked a bit alarmed by the number of shapes moving in the water around them. "Dr. Zelenka has modified the jumper's cloak so that we can display patterns of light and electrical signals that are similar to the communication of the squid."

"And we're not getting the same kind of interference as long as we're using it as a movie projector," Lorne said. "It's when we switch it over to producing a shield that things get screwy."

"So we should be able to use it to talk to these creatures," Lynn continued. "However, right now we'd simply be guessing at any meaning we were conveying. I need a bigger sample of the language of the squid for the Stargate translation program to begin to work."

"I don't know that we want to try talking to them until we're sure what we'd be saying," Lorne said.

"I agree that might be unwise," Teyla said. "Were you able to decipher any words the creatures might understand from the data you collected earlier?"

"This cluster here —" Lynn turned his tablet to display a series of flashing colors and movements from the squid that Elizabeth could just identify as repeating between a series of video clips. "This might be referring to the Ancients themselves."

"Or to humans in general?" Elizabeth suggested. "Telling them that we're humans might be a good starting point."

"They are most likely aware of that from their observations," Teyla said. "But it might show them that we're attempting to use their form of communication in a meaningful way."

"Let's try it," Elizabeth said. "At least we may be able to get some kind of response that way."

They'd been fortunate so far that in most of their tense first contacts with alien civilizations, they'd at least been able to speak a common language. If the builders of the Stargate system had intended for that to ensure understanding and respect between peoples, it hadn't quite worked out as planned. But it had meant that it was possible to introduce themselves and to negotiate without starting by working out a language to negotiate in.

Lynn had connected his tablet to the jumper's control panel with a cable, and his hands were moving over it swiftly. "All right, let's see what the squid think about this."

The reaction outside the jumper was immediate. The squid, who had been swimming in complex patterns around one another, now approached the jumper. Elizabeth counted two dozen of them, and wasn't certain how many more there might be. One long, tentacled form blended into another as the creatures swooped through the water, crossing in front of the jumper, their colors shifting and changing as they moved.

"This is good," Lynn said. "I'm getting a lot of additional data."

Teyla frowned at the creatures. "They are approaching the jumper very closely."

"I expect they're curious about what we're —" Lynn broke off as the jumper rocked. "All right, what was that?"

One of the squid rushed the jumper, its beak thumping against the jumper's side, sending another heavy jolt through the craft.

"We're probably structurally sound enough not to worry about this," Elizabeth said. "Right?"

"The jumpers are pretty sturdy, although I don't think we've ever actually tried to measure how tentacle-proof they are," Lorne said. "But I'm not going anywhere fast, unless I plow through them."

"No, no, no, don't do that," Lynn said urgently. "The

translation program is getting somewhere, I think."

One of the squid barreled into another, forcing it away from the jumper. Another hit the jumper hard, and Elizabeth took a firm grip on her seat. Its arms and tentacles splayed across the forward window, and the jumper tilted off-balance.

"Can you keep us steady?" Lynn asked testily.

Lorne rolled his eyes. "Would you like to come up here and try to compensate for being grabbed by a kraken?"

"I think classically the kraken is supposed to be an octopus," Elizabeth said.

"It depends on who you ask," Lynn said, "there's some speculation —"

"Whoa!" Lorne exclaimed, as one of the squid rammed the jumper with its beak with a resounding bang. It swirled around, heading in for another pass. "I may have to try to disengage —"

"Wait," Teyla said. Two other creatures slammed into the one heading for them from the side, ramming it out of the way and enveloping it in their arms. The patterns they were flashing looked a lot like the pattern that Lynn thought meant "Ancient" or "human," although they were growing brighter with electrical energy, and there was no telling what that meant.

The knot of arms and tentacles pulled apart and reformed as the creatures struggled. Something dark stained the water, and whether that was blood or some kind of ink, Elizabeth was afraid that the confrontation outside the jumper was growing violent.

"Can we pull back?" she asked.

"Negative, ma'am," Lorne said. "We're right in the middle of them."

"There appear to be two separate groups of the creatures," Teyla said. "One attacking the jumper, and the other attempting to prevent them from harming us." Vast bodies roiled in the water, with the imposing size of Earth dolphins or small whales paired with a sinuous grace that allowed them to bend and change direction as no creature with bones could have. More dark fluid stained the blue sea.

"Or trying to prevent them from harming themselves by attacking a metal ship," Elizabeth said. "I'm just not sure it's working. Moving away may be the least destructive option after all."

"Dr. Weir, look," Teyla said, and Elizabeth returned her attention to the forward screens. Outside the jumper, the altercation between the creatures seemed to have ended in most of them backing away. They swirled in two distinct groups, the color patterns on their sides shifting rapidly. One of the largest individuals approached the jumper, and Elizabeth braced herself for another jolt, but it only hung there in the water, its colors changing in repetitive patterns.

"Dr. Lynn," Elizabeth said. "Now would be a good time."

"I think I've got it," Lynn said. "Colonel Lorne, if you can patch this through the jumper's communication system so that we can run this through the city's computers, I think I can synthesize a voice so that we can hear what they're saying."

"On it," Lorne said. "Here goes."

After a few moments a computer-generated voice said, "You are the Ancients." The voice sounded female, although that might not reflect anything more than a default setting. "Are you the Ancients? You have returned. You have returned?"

"It's having some trouble distinguishing statements from questions, I think," Lynn said. "The translation should improve as my algorithms incorporate more data. Talking will help."

Elizabeth cleared her throat. "We are humans from the city of Atlantis."

"The city of Atlantis? The city of Atlantis. The city of the Ancients."

"Yes, the city of the Ancients," Teyla said.

"We have brought the city of the Ancients to this planet, to live here," Elizabeth said. "We mean you no harm."

There was a clamor of voices, accompanied by flashing colors from both groups.

"You came here through the Stargate," the same voice said. "Did you come here through the Stargate?"

"We came here through space," Elizabeth said. "Not through the Stargate." She wasn't sure that concept would be comprehensible to a creature that lived its entire life under the ocean.

"The cold void between the worlds," the voice said, somewhat to her surprise.

"Yes, that's right. I'm Elizabeth Weir," she said. "The other one of us who is speaking is Teyla Emmagen."

"I don't understand those words," the creature said.

Elizabeth looked at Lynn, who paused the communication link. "Their language appears to be entirely visual," he said. "If they have names, they're probably distinctive color patterns or forms of movements."

"Those are our names," Elizabeth said. "I don't think we can render them into your language."

"I am…" There was a flashing series of colors in a kind of rippling swirl.

"I'm afraid we can't say that, either," Elizabeth said. "The way that we are able to speak to you only works for ordinary words."

"Old Hunter," the creature said. "You can call me that. It is something like the name they call me, now. After so long here. And you have returned? You have returned. Where is the one called Janus? Has he returned with you?"

"All right, that's extremely interesting," Lynn said, pausing the communication link again. "It looks to me like what they're literally saying is something like 'the passage goes in two directions' — a reasonable translation of 'archway' for underwater creatures, which is of course one of the literal meanings of 'Janus' — in any event, my point is that the Atlantis computers are translating that phrase with confidence as the word 'Janus.' If that was their name for him, it's been preserved in their language for a long time."

"The Ancients have not returned with us," Elizabeth said. "Most of them are dead long ago. Do your people still have stories about the Ancients?"

Patterns rippled down the creature's side. "I remember the Ancients," the creature said. "They brought me to this world, long ago."

"That was thousands of years ago," Elizabeth said.

"Thousands? Thousands. Yes. We were always long-lived, my folk. We lived in bright seas, warm seas. We hunted together and told stories of the hunting. There was no ice on our world. Only the ocean and the people and food for the hunting. Then he came, Janus. I remember Janus. I was there."

Elizabeth looked at Teyla in skeptical surprise. Teyla looked equally surprised but shrugged as if to say that the longevity of giant squid wasn't one of her areas of expertise.

Lynn cut off the communications yet again. "I'm no biologist, but that sounds improbable."

"But not impossible," Elizabeth said. "We've certainly met Wraith who've survived since the time of the Ancients. Even since the creation of the first Wraith."

"Janus brought us here," Old Hunter said. "We, those who came, we were smaller. We were young then. We had learned to speak to the Ancients, the humans, who lived on our world, with colors, simple words. He wanted to know about us, about our lives and how our bodies worked. He brought us here in one of the great ships of the Ancients. He said he would teach us many secrets. That we would learn together how to become like those who depart to become spirit in the sea that cannot be reached."

"To become like Ascended beings," Elizabeth said.

"Some of us had become such," Old Hunter said. "Dreamed and learned until they left this sea for that other one, without leaving a body behind. He thought we could have their power without leaving the sea that we knew. But we did all leave the warm sea of our child-hood, we came here to this world, and it was cold, more cold than we had ever imagined the sea could become. We suffered, but we are strong, we did not die. We were proud of our endurance, we worked hard to learn what Janus could teach."

"We have heard of Janus's experiments," Teyla said. "He manipulated the genes of my own ancestors as well, trying to make us more like Ascended beings without leaving physical existence. In the process, he created the Wraith."

"I don't understand that word."

Elizabeth raised an eyebrow at Lorne.

"I guess none of what we've been through really registered under water," Lorne said. "I mean, what would they have seen, here? Our ships, coming and going, but they wouldn't have known about our problem."

"The Wraith hunt humans," Teyla said. "They must, to survive, except for a few who have found a way that they can survive without killing the humans they feed on, and that is very new. They were an attempt to create humans — Ancients — who would be more like the Ancients who had ascended, without requiring them to follow a path of spiritual discipline. It was an unfortunate short cut. Instead, Janus created a species with some of the powers of the Ascended Ancients, but with the need to feed on the life energy of others."

"This has caused problems," Weir said dryly.

"Janus tried to change us, but it did not happen as he hoped," Old Hunter said. "We had always been long-lived compared to others like us on our world, animals who did not speak. That was one of the things that interested him about us. After he changed us, we lived longer still, maybe longer even than he expected. Those he changed, and our spawn, do not ever die from old age, only from accident or disease. Some of us who remember those days still live, though we are few now."

"This happened to the Wraith, too," Teyla said. "Perhaps these experiments were similar."

"But we did not gain the ability to speak without sight or change our bodies, or the other things he hoped for us. And in time he said he could go no farther, that we were not enough like the Ancients for him to make the change in us."

"At which point he decided to experiment on my ancestors instead," Teyla said.

"What happened after that?" Elizabeth asked. "Did those of you who had come to this planet decide not to return to your homeworld?"

"We debated what to do. Some wanted to return home, but Janus said that would be difficult. We had grown large, and difficult for him to transport. He said that he would return us in time, and we saw no need to hurry him. But he went away, and others came and went, and then they all went and did not return. We called to them, we waited, we went back to the island where they had lived, but there were only beasts that did not speak left there, and the Ancients were gone."

"That would be when the Wraith took over the Ancient installation and killed their captors," Teyla said. "It must have seemed to your people that they simply disappeared."

"But now you have come back," the creature said. "You bring the great ship."

"The city of Atlantis," Elizabeth said. "Yes."

"Janus spoke of the city of Atlantis. Now it has come. And other ships. We have felt the vibrations of their landing and their rising. We have seen lights moving above the water unlike the movement of the sun."

"The ships of our people," Elizabeth said. "Yes. We mean to live on this planet, but we have no desire to harm any of you, just as we would like for you not to cause harm to us or to our city, the great ship. If we are hurting you in some way by being here, please tell us, and we will do whatever we can to fix the problem. We would like to be your friends."

"You did not ask to be our friends when you arrived," Old Hunter said, shifting in the water to fix them with first one eye and then the other. "You did not ask our permission to hunt and live in these waters."

"We did not know that your people were intelligent beings who we could talk to," Teyla said. "Now that we know that, we can begin again."

"We realized that you were intelligent from watching your communication with each other," Elizabeth said. "We have noticed that you have been gathering in unusually large groups in the area around the city in the last few days. Is this a normal time for your people to gather? Are we in the way of some kind of migration or mating ritual?"

"Normal? No, not normal. We have called for all of us who will come to assemble, because you have returned. We still remember the warm waters, the waters filled with food. Some of us remember. We remember Janus's promise. And now you have come back. You will take us back to our first world, take us home."

"Is that what you would like us to do?" Elizabeth asked.

"Some of us. Many of us. Others know only this world, and fear to leave it. We have told each shoal that they must decide, together, what they will do. Some of the shoals have decided they will leave, to return to our first home. Others will stay. Some shoals have been unable to resolve their disagreements, and no longer swim together. I regret this. But most of us are reaching decisions. And most of us — with some exceptions —" The squid turned and pointed in a nearly human gesture toward the group of squid who had tried to attack the jumper. "— have agreed that those who want to go will not be stopped."

Elizabeth took a moment to phrase her response carefully. "We would like to help you," she said. "But we need to figure out what's actually feasible."

Lynn shrugged. "Not in my wheelhouse," he murmured.

"We need time to talk about how to accomplish this," Elizabeth said. "And we will have to figure out how to locate your original world."

"That question I can answer," the creature said. "Visnareth Asnivan." It sounded like a name at first.

"Ah," Lynn said, and Elizabeth followed his gaze to the viewscreen. Across the creature's side, patterns of dots and lines repeated the same six familiar symbols.

"That's a gate address, isn't it?"

"It is indeed, and the translation program is helpfully translating each symbol into the Ancient syllable it represents. As in the Milky Way galaxy, most local populations use names for worlds that have nothing to do with the gate designation, but in a visual language, the gate designation is a lovely and logical ways of preserving the name of the planet."

"We did not have a name for our homeworld, before the Ancients came," the creature said. "But this we learned, when they taught us about the stars and their places in the great sea of space, and the archways that led between them. This I remembered here, and taught my descendants, in case I no longer lived when the Ancients returned to us with their ships. It is our way home."

Home. The computerized voice had little inflection, but the word still tugged at Elizabeth's heart. She wondered if she would ever actually set foot on Earth again. She'd taken that risk when she came through the Stargate for the first time, but she hadn't expected home to be a quick gate trip away, and yet forbidden to her because of her state of existential limbo.

"We'll do everything we can," she said.

"In the meantime, try to keep everyone away from the city if you can," Lorne said. He glanced at Elizabeth in a silent question about how much more to say. It wasn't necessarily a good thing for the creatures to know that it was possible for them to bring the shield down.

"It's possible that your people could be hurt if they run into the force field that protects our city," Elizabeth said. "And something about the way you communicate using electricity is interfering with some of our systems. This is causing problems for us, and it would be helpful to us if you could move a little farther away from the city."

"I will ask, but I do not know how many will listen to me," the creature said. "They are absorbed in their choices, and their hope drives them to linger here, or their pain. There are some of us who are very angry that this decision has become necessary. They grieve because their mates or children are leaving them. They feel it would be better if you had never come back to this world."

"Unfortunately, we have," Elizabeth said. "Whatever decisions your people make now, we're here, and it may be possible for us to transport some of your people back to your original world. But please try to be patient while we figure out if this can be done and how to do it."

CHAPTER FOUR

"HAVE YOU lost your minds?" Rodney asked.

"That's not a technical recommendation, McKay," John said. Elizabeth and Dr. Lynn had returned full of enthusiasm for some kind of squid repatriation program, for which both Rodney and Radek were currently exhibiting significantly less enthusiasm. "Should I take that as 'it's not going to be possible,' or 'it's not going to be easy'?"

"It is certainly not going to be easy," Radek said. "The problem is that the gate is not in the water."

"They know that," Rodney said.

"I am just establishing the parameters. The gate will not operate when submerged, and even if it were partially submerged, that would require partially submerging the entire city with the shields down, which would cause prohibitive amounts of damage."

"I'm glad that we've ruled out flooding all our equipment and living space," Rodney said.

"Well, we could do it, in an emergency —" He waved a hand to cut off Rodney's sputtering response. "— but this is not an emergency, so, no, we will not do that. It might conceivably be possible to construct some kind of conduit from the water to the Stargate, insert one end into the event horizon while it is still sealed to water, and then allow the squid to pass through, separate the module that goes through the Stargate, and allow it to be transmitted —"

"Or we could just use a spaceship," John said. "Right? Rather than building a big squid monorail through the main control room?"

"No," Rodney said.

"Maybe," Radek said. They looked at each other, apparently conducting a silent argument by means of eyebrow movements.

"The problem is the water," Rodney said. "You'd be talking about filling the cargo holds with water and squid, which, even granting that we could probably make the cargo holds water-tight given a tremendous amount of work in a shipyard back on Earth, is going to be a tremendous amount of mass for the ships to haul. It's maybe doable in theory. In practice it's a terrible idea."

"Wouldn't we need filtration equipment for the water, too?" Elizabeth asked.

"Probably," Radek said. "We are talking about a journey of several days. The biologists would have a better idea of what specific temperature and water quality would be required."

"You're talking about building a massive saltwater aquarium, and either installing it on several different ships, or making several trips," Rodney said. "This is not something you throw together in ten minutes to put some goldfish in."

"We could do it," Radek said.

"At the cost of a lot of time and a lot of money," Rodney said. "Maybe I'm underestimating the IOA's commitment to the pursuit of happiness among

Pegasus-galaxy invertebrates, but I don't think they're going to be willing to pay for this."

"Well, we've got to do something," Elizabeth said. "To begin with, we need the creatures to move away from Atlantis, and they're not going to do that while they think we're their only way home. We have to weigh the expense of whatever solution we come to against the danger and expense of potentially having to move the city to another planet."

"Let's try not to do that again," John said. "Even if we might get better weather."

"I'd rather not, no. But beyond that, we opened up this can of worms by arriving and opening the question of returning to their homeworld. They're already experiencing violent conflict on the subject. If we refuse to help them, there may be serious breaches between groups of the creatures if they blame one another. Or, which may be even more likely, they'll blame us."

"And if they do?" John asked.

"We're going to lose the shields entirely in a couple of days," Rodney said. "If they don't know that the shield power is dropping, they're still going to notice when the shields go down. And right now we're burning through ZPM power trying to keep the shields up as long as we can."

"Which is also expensive," Elizabeth said. "You could even make the argument that it's more expensive, since ZPM power isn't replenishable."

"If we take the shields down, they can tear up the underside of the city," Radek said. "Probably not major damage, but inconvenient and potentially dangerous.

And we have biology teams who will not appreciate being confined to the city if we're not able to lower the shields to let people in and out."

"We could ask the IOA," Elizabeth said. "I think if we put the spaceship option to them the right way—"

"They'll still say no," John said. "Because that's the right answer. We're talking about spending a lot of IOA money and Air Force resources and personnel time to refit a ship to carry a bunch of civilians who, you have to admit, aren't in any immediate danger."

"This world isn't ideal for their needs."

"This world isn't ideal for our needs, and yet we're here," John said. "When I complain about the cold, McKay tells me to put on a sweater."

"It's not as cold as Antarctica," Rodney said. "It's not even as cold as Canada. Just because we were all spoiled by living somewhere warm and nice, for a while…"

"The squid can't exactly put on a sweater," Elizabeth said.

"No, but they're surviving here. They're breeding, they have food, and I can't honestly tell the IOA that we should spend a lot of money rescuing them rather than spending that money rescuing the next group of people who are actually in trouble."

"Janus promised to return them, and then he didn't follow through. I think we bear some kind of responsibility for repairing the mistakes of the people whose city we've inherited, rather than just shooting the people they've wronged because they're inconvenient to us."

"Yes, and I never said we were going to do that," John said. "I just said I think the spaceship option is out.

McKay and Zelenka. How hard would it be to make the cargo compartment in one of the jumpers watertight without relying on the shield to hold the water in?"

Radek and Rodney exchanged looks again. "Relatively easy," Radek said. "You do not want to use the shield to do that anyway, because the shield is projected outside the jumper. If the water leaks as far as the shield, that means that it has already gone through the cargo compartment and is risking shorting out the control crystals or the jumper's wiring. But making it watertight, that is just a matter of building an inner compartment, essentially—"

"Like turning a car into an aquarium," John said. "I saw that on HGTV."

"Why do we have HGTV?" Elizabeth asked.

"It came with the databurst," John said. He found it less easy to explain why he'd been watching it, except that it had been very late at night, but she didn't seem inclined to ask.

"We can do it," Radek said. "But, still, the filtration system—"

"Isn't going to matter, because in the jumper, we can use the Stargate, so the whole trip isn't going to take more than a few minutes," John said. "We need to do some recon anyway, and make sure we're not sending these folks to a world that's been overrun by the Wraith or where the oceans all boiled away thousands of years ago. Let's refit the jumper, pick up a squid volunteer, and go check it out. If it looks good, we can ferry their people through one by one whenever we have time."

"We can do that," Radek said.

"In the meantime, I'll get Lorne to take Teyla and Ronon to go take a preliminary look around and rule out big obvious problems."

"Like the Wraith," Elizabeth said dryly.

"Like the Wraith." He nodded to Radek and Ronon to dismiss them. Elizabeth stayed behind, watching him with her head to one side. "What?" he asked, when she didn't immediately speak.

"It's disconcerting," she said. "I always had tremendous respect for our military personnel, because we wouldn't have survived a day in the Pegasus Galaxy without military support. We were all on the same team. But at the root of it, we were a scientific expedition, even if we were a scientific expedition under siege, and we never hesitated to push for all the Air Force resources we could get. That's changed since I was gone."

"Carter was the best replacement for you when you were..." He trailed off, unsure what the best way of putting it was.

"Temporarily dead?"

"Something most people don't have to say very often, but, yeah, that. She had the experience, we were in a bad tactical situation at that point, and frankly nobody else wanted the job. I think they should have left her in charge, but when they kicked her back to Earth and we got Woolsey, things swung back the other way. Maybe that was a good thing in some ways. The Air Force is never going to be anything other than the Air Force. The expedition is more flexible when we're under civilian leadership. But... here we are."

"You deserve this command," Elizabeth said. "And

I don't want you to think for a minute that I believe I ought to have it back."

"Nothing's final about who's in charge. I think it ought to be you. But right now it's me. And as much as I can't believe I'm worrying about the Air Force's budget, that's part of my job now."

"It happens to all of us at some point," Elizabeth said. "Responsibility."

"Was I chronically irresponsible, when you first knew me?" The words came out a little more sharply than he meant for them to. He wasn't sure that had ever exactly been his problem.

"You shot Dr. McKay when we'd been here a week," she pointed out.

"He asked me to," he said. It was a familiar joke, and it helped to ease the sense that they were on unexpectedly unfamiliar ground. He was used to people disappearing from his life suddenly and without warning. He wasn't sure he'd ever get used to them coming back, no matter how much he preferred it.

He wasn't sure he'd ever get used to not going out on every mission with the team, either — his team, he wasn't about to stop calling them. It wasn't that he doubted that Teyla, Ronon, and Rodney could check out an alien planet without him babysitting them, but it made him twitchy to be stuck back in Atlantis behaving himself and not taking risks. He didn't relax until Lorne's jumper reappeared through the iris and he had the team in the conference room to debrief.

"So, what have we got?" he asked once they were settled there again.

"Lots of water," Ronon said. "And some islands."

"Basically that," Rodney said. "Atmosphere is breathable, if damp. It's pretty similar to the atmosphere here, and the squishy sciences people think it shouldn't pose any problems for the squid. Which we probably shouldn't keep calling them if they're an intelligent species."

"Janus appears to have referred to them using the Ancient word that translates as 'squid,'" Teyla said. "He does not seem to have been particularly interested in the culture of his experimental subjects."

And he had experimented on Teyla's ancestors, thus landing the galaxy with a nasty, Wraith-sized problem. John was still inclined to treat the squid with caution as a result, although he had to admit that so far they seemed like perfectly nice, non-lifesucking people who just happened to have tentacles.

"The gate is on an island," Ronon said. "In the middle of a bunch of ruins. There are a lot more ruins underwater. Looks like there were human inhabitants who had industry at one point. Steel girders, broken glass."

"My guess is that the island used to be part of a much larger continent, but in the last couple of thousand years, the ice caps melted, the sea level rose, and eventually some islands were all that was left," Rodney said. "The human population probably decamped before that, at the point where their agricultural land, mining, whatever they depended on to support cities was all underwater. They're lucky they had a gate they could reach, not an orbital gate that would have left them stuck there."

"Perhaps the Ancients intended to monitor the planet

and help its inhabitants in the event of such a change," Teyla said. "But when it came, the Ancients were no longer there."

"Well, we're here, so let's see what we can do," John said.

***

The first obstacle they encountered was that try as they might, Old Hunter wouldn't fit in the converted jumper. While her body was flexible up to a point, and her beak and body fit inside the cargo compartment, her attempts to squeeze her tentacles and arms in as well resulted only in murky fluctuations of color that the translator interpreted as grunts of pain and in alarming creaking noises from the jumper's inner struts. One saucer-sized, unblinking eye was pressed against the new transparent partition between the passenger compartment and the cargo hold, an unnerving view.

"McKay —" John began.

McKay gave the eye an unhappy look. "Can I refit the jumper with an expanded cargo compartment? Sure, if you don't particularly care about long-term structural integrity. I wouldn't take it into space, or anything, especially not with the shield unreliable at best —"

"I'm not planning to."

"But, as I was about to say, I can't do it while we're out here in the water. We can either go back to Atlantis and spend a couple of days refitting, or you can find a smaller squid."

"Old Hunter?" John asked. "What do you want to do?"

The squid knotted her arms in an unhappy posture. "I am eager to see the world of my birth again," she said.

"But my people are nervous about this great change in our lives, and some of them are very angry at the decisions that have been made. I am afraid that they will fight each other, and that some will try to attack the city of Atlantis, despite your energy shields."

"That would be a bad idea," John said.

"That is what I am afraid of. I will send my descendent instead. He is called…" She displayed a much simpler pattern than her own name, made up of bold stripes. John might have been able to replicate it with a marker and a sheet of paper, but he couldn't very well say it.

"Okay," John said. "Let's call him Stripes."

A considerably smaller squid came forward.

"I am ready to go! We will see another world! I will be the first of my people to go there! They will remember my name for ever and ever!"

Rodney and Ronon both rolled their eyes. Teyla looked amused. John was reminded of Torren, and wondered just how old the squid was. In any event, he fit neatly into the cargo hold, and John was able to close the doors and activate their makeshift filtration system.

"Everything comfy back there?"

"Perfect! What do all these things do?" The squid poked at a cargo compartment, opening and closing it repeatedly.

"Please don't touch anything," Rodney said.

"I cannot not touch anything! I am always touching the water!" The squid flushed a bright orange color that John suspected reflected amusement.

"Everybody keep their tentacles inside the vehicle," John said. "Here we go."

They cut a swift course through the water, erupting out of the waves into the air a careful distance away from the large group of squid who were circling the city. A high-pitched noise of excitement emanated through the jumper's speakers as it broke the surface of the water, and the jumper shuddered as the squid's tentacles thrashed.

"Let's not get too excited back there," John said. "If this thing comes apart in mid-air, you're not going to like it."

He brought the jumper in through the ceiling entrance and slowed it to hover in front of the gate.

"All right down there?" Elizabeth asked.

"We're fine," John said. "Let's just get there before our guest gets his tentacles in a knot."

"That is not possible!" Stripes said cheerfully. "Are all of these creatures air-breathers? How do they move around in the air? Why don't they fall down?"

"Why would we fall down?" Ronon asked.

"Lt. Salawi, dial the gate," Elizabeth said.

The iris boiled blue in front of the jumper. "Is that water?" the squid asked.

"That is the Stargate," Teyla said. "It will transport us to the home of your ancestors."

"Through a tube!" the creature said happily.

"No, it's a wormhole, which, technically… yeah, okay, it's a tube," Rodney said. "We're not doing particle physics for aquatic civilizations today, though. Unless you're really interested, in which case…"

"They're not," Ronon said.

"Another time," John said. "Hang onto… well, just

brace yourself." He threaded the needle of the gate, and subspace swirled around the jumper as they raced toward their destination. He expected an excited clamor, but awe seemed to have replaced manic interest, and the squid was plastered against the transparent barrier, turning first one fist-sized eye and then the other to see out the viewscreen.

They burst out again into sunlight. Below them, a plaza still paved with cracked and weathered stones was surrounded by the ruins of a city, walls crumbled and roofs torn away by past storms. The ruins descended into the water, where rolling waves broke against the remains of walls or lapped against beaches that might have been made of crumbled stone and brick. The water was a clear, tropical green, and beneath it the sunken city looked like a scuba diver's paradise.

"Wonder if there's anything interesting down there," Rodney said.

"More squid, I hope," John said. "Let's get out past these ruins — unless your people would use them for, I don't know, nesting or something?"

"We bear live young! We do not hide eggs among structures! We might come to a place like this because it was interesting, or to teach the very young." The tips of its tentacles writhed against the barrier. "But we must have open water to hunt. We travel long distances when we hunt! Many, many kilometers."

John assumed that last represented an Ancient measure of distance, and wondered how the squid measured it. "All right. Let's get out into the open water and see what life signs we can pick up."

The sun sparkled off the water as they cleared the ruins of the city. It really did look like an ideal vacation spot. He wondered if the commander of Atlantis ever got a vacation, and suspected he knew the answer. All the more reason not to take the job on a permanent basis, although if the IOA decided they couldn't trust Elizabeth, he wasn't sure he wanted anyone else to have it, either. Carter had been good, and Woolsey had been a lot better than they'd originally feared, but who knew what they'd get saddled with next time.

"So, are we planning to look for the squid in the air, or…" Rodney prompted.

"I thought we'd submerge," John said, pointing the nose of the jumper down toward the water and telling himself to focus on the problems of the day.

The water was clearer than the chill waters near Atlantis, and rich with life. Colorful schools of fish darted by, and John had to swerve more than once to avoid hitting larger fish that trundled by at a more sober speed.

"The trick is going to be picking out any particular kind of life sign," he said.

"Let me out! I want to see! All these fish look tasty!"

"You should be careful," Teyla warned. "You do not know if some of these fish might be harmful for you to eat."

"They did not hurt my ancestors," the squid grumbled.

"Or perhaps some did, and you have not learned to avoid them," Teyla pointed out. "One of the first things that you must learn when you travel through the Stargate is to be careful of unknown plants and animals." It was exactly the same tone of voice she used to talk to Torren, and John had to repress a smile.

"Over there," Ronon said, pointing to something that flashed past the viewscreen at a distance. "That looked like it might have been one of these guys."

John sent the jumper in that direction, willing the schools of fish to get out of the way rather than stun themselves against the jumper's hull. Maybe they needed to paint the jumpers brighter colors for underwater use, something that screamed "move it, we're coming through."

"There!" Teyla exclaimed. "I see it. John, turn to two o'clock."

The squid were hunting, harrying a school of fish through the water and picking off stragglers. As he watched, they slowed, forming a close knot in the water and devouring their kill.

"Okay," he said. "We're going to let you out here. Keep your distance until you're sure these guys are friendly." He figured he'd let Stripes do the talking at first, rather than trusting in the communication program that Lynn had installed in the jumper.

"Of course they will be friendly," Stripes said. "They are our own kin!"

"Yes, I wish it worked like that, but it really doesn't always," Rodney said. "You should meet my parents. Just stay back far enough that you can run away if they turn out not to like strangers, all right?"

"If you say so," Stripes said. John released the cargo bay doors with a certain degree of misgiving. He planned to keep his distance himself. There were too many of them for the shield to be of any use if they got close, and John didn't like the idea of the jumper being vulnerable to attack, especially not underwater. He'd come to rely on the little ships' near-indestructability, one gift of the Ancients that had come without the usual unfortunate strings on their leftover technology.

The young squid arrowed directly toward the strangers, stopping closer than John hoped he would, but far enough away from them that he was in clear view from the jumper. John brought the jumper around to an angle that he hoped would let him bring it between Stripes and the strangers if the meeting turned unpleasant.

"Hello, other people!" the squid said, his whole body flashing with excitement. "I am from another ocean! My people come from your people! I am home!"

The squid flashed bright patterns in return, but the jumper's computer didn't provide audio.

"Is this thing working?" John said. "Maybe we should have brought Lynn with us."

"I am from another place!" the squid said. "We should be friends!"

"I am from another place," one of the squid repeated, and then flashed an assortment of patterns that once again didn't translate. "We should. From your." Then more untranslatable flashing. It was followed by purposeful movement, the squid taking up a formation that resembled their hunting posture a lot more than it did the loose grouping they'd rested in to eat.

"Stripes, I think you should get some distance," John said.

"I don't understand you, other people!" Stripes said.

"You're not making sense."

"Not making! From another place! I am!" The patterns were jumbled echoes of those Stripes had used, trailing off into muddied swirls of blue and green, but the computer gave them an angry intonation.

"I agree with Colonel Sheppard," Teyla said firmly. "You should return to the jumper now."

Two of the squid moved as one toward Stripes, veering toward him from two directions, and he raced away in alarm. John angled the jumper's cargo bay doors toward him, and he dived through, his beak hitting the partition between the cargo compartment and the passenger compartment with a heavy thump.

"Careful!" Rodney exclaimed. "If you crack that, we're all going to have problems."

"Let's get out of the water. Except for you." John closed the doors behind Stripes and brought the jumper swiftly up to the surface.

"I don't understand," the squid said mournfully as John leveled the jumper out above the shining waves. "They aren't speaking properly. It looks like words, but I don't understand what they're saying."

CHAPTER FIVE

"I HAVE A theory," Lynn said. He and Elizabeth had come through the Stargate after John's report had made it clear that establishing contact with the squid on their home planet wasn't going to be as easy as they'd thought. Stripes was currently exploring the shallow water near the island, having been sternly warned not to venture out into the open water where his fellow creatures lived. Elizabeth perched on a weathered stone wall, enjoying the warm breeze. She missed having the city of Atlantis in a temperate location, although she appreciated that the team hadn't had a lot of choices when they returned it to the Pegasus Galaxy.

"Your program isn't working?" Rodney asked.

"It's working to translate the language of these squid, which is a variant of Ancient," Lynn said. "From what Old Hunter said, this is a language they learned specifically to communicate with the humans on their planet. It's possible that their original language was more distantly based on Ancient — I'm not sure whether these creatures evolved naturally or were seeded here by the Ancients, and I don't think it's possible to know that without a great deal of genetic research we don't have time for right now."

"But your point is?" John prompted.

"My point is, whatever language these squid speak now, it's evolved over thousands of years. Remember,

Janus altered their genetic makeup to make them more long-lived. Their ancestors must have had much shorter life-spans. They've had hundreds or thousands of generations for their language to change. If it has Ancient roots at all, it's experienced significant drift, and without visitors through the Stargate, there hasn't been any stabilizing factor as there has been for the human populations of the Pegasus Galaxy."

"So what can we do?" Elizabeth said. "I'm reluctant to return them to this planet and put them next to resident populations they can't talk to."

"I think more data will help," Lynn said. "If I make enough observations of the language that's spoken here and compare it to the data I originally collected, I may be able to pin down patterns of drift that would allow us to at least assemble a basic vocabulary. But I can't do that in ten minutes."

"At least that would let us get an idea of whether the squid here have any interest in sharing their world with strangers," Elizabeth said. "I think we have the time. Colonel Sheppard?"

"I think you're right," John said. "I'd like us to keep our distance given that we don't have shields, but we should be able to maneuver close enough to get some video and back off if they start getting testy. Ronon, McKay, you can go on back through. I can hang out here for a while and let Dr. Lynn film his squid."

"Thank you for recognizing that this is not a physics-related problem," Rodney said, heading for the DHD.

"You're sure you're good?" Ronon asked.

"Yes," John said. "We'll yell for help if we need it."

"I wouldn't mind a tour around the island," Elizabeth said. It felt good to be somewhere that wasn't Atlantis for a while. As much as she loved the city, she did miss Earth, and this felt very much like one of many tropical areas where she'd vacationed and worked in the past.

"I will stay as well," Teyla said.

"All right, all aboard," John said.

Underwater, John took the jumper out past the ruins, and they made a slow circle around the island, diverting to follow groups of the squid as they hunted and participated in whatever other activities made up their day. It was frustrating to know that they were talking without being able to understand, but Elizabeth watched all the same, hoping that the shifting colors and lines written across their skins would resolve themselves into meaningful patterns. After a while, she traded places with Teyla to take the front passenger seat while Teyla went back to look over Lynn's shoulder while he worked.

"Ever think about becoming a wildlife photographer?" she asked John as he followed a group of hunting squid, tilting the jumper to get a better angle for their recordings.

"It would probably help to be able to take good pictures using an actual camera," John said. "And, no. I always wanted to fly. Although I didn't really expect submarines to be my thing."

"Submarines in space," Elizabeth said. "I don't think you lose your Air Force mojo for that." She watched as a group of squid passed fish back and forth, wondering what the significance was. "My career ambitions were never as clear-cut. No one starts kindergarten saying 'I want to run an NGO,' let alone 'I want to lead an expedition to another planet.'"

"Both of which you've done," he pointed out.

"And now... what?"

"What do you want to do?"

"Well, now that we're not dealing with a Wraith attack fleet or rogue Asgard —" She broke off as the jumper's heads-up display flashed an insistent message. "Don't tell me."

"I'm picking up transmissions," John said. "Some kind of radio signal. Definitely not produced by our friends here."

"It's not out of the realm of possibility that a species could evolve to communicate using radio waves," Elizabeth said.

"Yes, but they're extremely unlikely to be an aquatic species," Lynn said. "Radio waves don't travel well through sea water."

"Yeah, I'm going to take us up so that we can get a clear signal," John said. The jumper plunged upward through the waves, leveling off a few meters above the water.

"— reporting in," a human voice said clearly. "We're bringing the submersible back to site B."

"Copy that," another voice said. "Any luck?"

"Nothing spectacular, but not a wasted day."

"Fair enough."

"That does not sound like squid," Teyla said.

"Can you zero in on the source of the signal?" Elizabeth asked.

"Way ahead of you," John said. "I just wish we could activate the cloak."

"We can't?"

"Not with the modifications McKay and Zelenka made. They've worked hard on getting the cloak to project visible light and those weird electrical signals the squid are using to communicate without frying itself. They'll have to take the control panels apart to undo everything they did."

"It's amazing how used you get to having invisible spaceships," Elizabeth said.

"We're so spoiled, it's true."

John brought the jumper in toward a moderately-sized island. Like the one where the gate was located, it had clearly once been covered in buildings, now tumbled and overgrown with vegetation that extended down to a beach of sand and weathered stone. Unlike the one where the gate was located, a fairly large boat was anchored offshore — it must have been brought through the Stargate in pieces, Elizabeth thought, as it couldn't possibly have fit through the iris — and beside it, an odd metal sphere with protruding pipes and wheels and what looked like articulated metal arms. It looked like a larger version of an old-fashioned diving bell, she decided, or some kind of very early submarine.

The men working near the boat, piling it with some kind of crates, wore familiar uniforms.

"Well, it's not the rogue Asgard," Elizabeth said.

"Just the Genii," John said. "Great."

"It may be best to avoid attracting their attention," Teyla said.

"Working on it," John said, bringing the jumper around in a circle and heading back toward the gate. "I'm not sure that there's anything we want to chat about right now."

The jumper's screen signaled an incoming transmission, and John switched on a crackling audio signal. "Atlantis ship, come in," a man said. "You are in Genii territory. We require that you land immediately and explain your presence here. We will consider failure to do so to indicate that your purpose is espionage. Atlantis ship, respond."

"Hi to you, too," John said. "This is Atlantis Jumper Two, Colonel Sheppard commanding. If you've got a flat place for us to land, we can come down and have a little talk."

"There is a cleared area thirty meters west of our boat," the man said. "We will expect you to land there directly."

"Do you think that is wise?" Teyla asked after John cut the transmission.

"We're not at war with the Genii," John said. "I'm not sure we're friends with the Genii, either, but I doubt these folks have the authority to start a war with Atlantis by kidnapping our people. I'm also not really prepared to accept their word for it that they own this planet, so I think we have some things to talk about."

"I'm all for talking," Elizabeth said. "But let's be on our guard."

"As if we were ever anything else in this galaxy," Lynn said. "Is there anyone we meet who consistently doesn't pose any threat to us?"

"The Athosians have always been friendly," Teyla

said. "But I would hardly say that we could never pose any threat."

"I wouldn't say that," John said.

They landed on a patch of ground between overgrown ruins. Several uniformed Genii stood at the edge of the field and waited for them to land, scowling up at the jumper. When they stepped out of the jumper, one of the Genii, who looked sunburned and swelteringly hot in his uniform, stepped forward to meet them.

"Atlantis team. Explain yourselves."

"Let's start with introductions," John said. "I'm Colonel Sheppard, acting commander in Atlantis. We're here on a survey mission. And you are…?"

"Captain Davon Minos," the man said. "In charge of Genii outpost 17."

"We weren't aware of one through sixteen," Elizabeth said.

"There's no reason you should be."

"This'll go a lot faster if you fill us in on what's going on," John said. "We're not trying to get in your way. We had no idea you were even here."

"We're conducting a salvage operation," Minos said.

"What did you lose?" John asked mildly.

"We haven't lost anything. The submerged parts of the city are full of valuable metals and plastics. We're retrieving them and transporting them back to our homeworld. We have divers in the water, and multiple boats out exploring various potential salvage sites."

"Okay," John said. "We don't have any interest in conducting salvage operations here. We're here to make contact with the planet's inhabitants."

"The planet is uninhabited," Minos said, frowning.

"I'm afraid that is not correct," Teyla said. "The planet is inhabited by an aquatic intelligent species. We have communicated with their relatives on another planet, and are in the process of establishing communication with the creatures here."

"You can't do that here," Minos said. "Whatever biological experiments you're doing, you'll have to do them somewhere else. We have exclusive salvage rights to this planet, and we're not interested in sharing it with the Atlantis mission."

"Now hang on just one second," Elizabeth said. "You don't own this planet. Its inhabitants do."

"You mean the 'aquatic intelligent species'? I'm sorry, you're going to have to persuade me that giant squid have rights. When they can sign a treaty, I'll be happy to talk."

"We could talk to Stripes about that," John said. "I bet those tentacles could hold a pen."

"We don't have time for playing around," Minos said. "Our position is that this planet does not contain any intelligent species. The squid may be smart animals, but that's all they are. Or do you claim to be able to translate their 'language'?"

"We're still working on that," John said.

"Right. But I'm not going to wait for them to succeed."

"What I believe Colonel Sheppard was about to say was that we have established contact with one of the creatures on our planet," Teyla said. "We can bring him here so that you can speak with him as well."

Minos wiped sweat from his forehead. "All right. Why

not? This should be entertaining. Go and get your squid."

"With your permission, Colonel Sheppard, I'll stay here while you do that," Elizabeth said. "I'm interested in the work you're doing here."

"I'll bet you are," Minos said. "But there's nothing here right now that's classified. Be our guest." He didn't point out that she'd just offered him a hostage against John and the jumper leaving without resolving the issue. John met her eyes skeptically, not needing to be told. She nodded imperceptibly, trying to communicate that this was important.

"All right," John said. "Teyla, you stay here with Elizabeth. I'll go get our tentacled friend."

"Let us just get our packs," Elizabeth said. As they stepped into the jumper, John swung himself into the pilot's seat.

"I hope you know what you're doing," he said.

"He called them squid, when all we'd said was 'intelligent aquatic species,'" Elizabeth said. "I think he knows more than he's letting on."

"Some of the workers reacted visibly to that part of the conversation as well," Teyla said. "Perhaps if you can distract Minos, I can speak with some of them and find out whether they have already encountered this world's indigenous life."

"Sounds like a plan," Elizabeth said. "We'll be fine, Colonel."

"I'll be back with a squid," John said.

"So," Elizabeth said, emerging with her most polite smile in place. "Show me what you're doing here."

It wasn't hard to pretend to be interested, although

the salvage operation involved ripping out scrap metal and other artifacts from the ocean floor in ways that would give an archaeologist back on Earth nightmares. Despite some prompting from her, Minos made it clear that he wasn't interested in the question of who had once lived here or how they had lived, only in the fact that what they had left behind could be useful to the Genii on their homeworld, where their technology had outstripped the availability of raw materials.

"We really didn't come here to salvage raw materials," she said.

"No. You have enough on your homeworld. Forgive me if I don't congratulate you."

"We have worked to develop our natural resources, and to conserve and reuse them. Sometimes more successfully than other times. Believe me, I sympathize with your need to find raw materials you can use."

She didn't add "especially since the Satedans showed you the door," but she was sure Minos was thinking it as well. The Genii had expected to be able to harvest ready-to-use metal from the ruins of Sateda for decades, but the return of the Satedans to their ancestral home had forced them to seek out new territory to explore. Unfortunately, like many previous explorers, the land they wanted to exploit actually belonged to someone else.

The jumper came into view, skimming the surface of the water, and settled on the beach, the waves lapping against its sides. John opened the cargo compartment into the sea, and Stripes burst out in a great splash of water and tentacles. The jumper raised off the ground

and backed out into deeper water until it could submerge again, and Stripes swam out to meet it.

"Here's our friend," Elizabeth said.

Minos shook his head. "This should be good for a
laugh."

As he stalked over to stand scowling at the ship and
the shadow of the squid just visible under the surface
of the water, Teyla came up behind Elizabeth.

"I have talked to several of the workers," she said.
"They have had troubling experiences with creatures
approaching them as they worked, especially in the
ruins that are in the deepest water. On more than one
occasion, they were attacked, and I have gotten the
strong impression that there have been deaths, or at
least injuries."

"Our tentacled friends?"

"It seems like a good bet. But it raises concerns, both
for the well-being of these squid, and for the squid back
on our own world. If the indigenous inhabitants are
hostile to strangers, that does not bode well for their
future."

"Well, these are their own descendants, not strangers."

"Will they believe it? If their generations are shorter,
any stories about Janus and the people he took away
with them may already have passed into legend."

"All right, let's do this, for what it's worth," John said
over the radio. Elizabeth switched the transmission
over to a handheld radio so that Minos could hear it
as well. "Stripes is one of the descendants of the squid
living here."

"You are more human people!" the squid said enthusiastically. "This is our planet! I have never seen it before!"

"This doesn't prove anything," Minos said. "That transmission could be from your ship."

"I'll be happy to show you my data and explain the translation software we've built," Lynn said from the jumper.

"No, thank you," Minos said.

"Stripes, can you swim up to the shore and show them stripes, then no stripes, then stripes?"

"That is easy, but why do you want me to say that?"

"Do me a favor," John said. The squid swam up obligingly, rolling in the shallow water to look unblinkingly up at Minos. His skin flashed from striped to solid to striped again. He raised one tentacle experimentally out of the water, poking at the boat, and Minos kicked it away.

"Hey," Elizabeth said.

"Please do not hurt our guest," Teyla said. "He is under our protection."

"Your trained animal, you mean," Minos said. "This is all very clever, and it might make an entertaining circus act back home, but I'm not about to grant that a creature who can't make a sound is an intelligent person."

"What would persuade you?" Elizabeth asked.

"Nothing," he said.

"I don't understand," Stripes said. "Is it a bargain? What are the terms?"

"No bargain, no deal, no negotiating with imaginary talking squid," Minos said, almost snarling. He looked hot and very uncomfortable, and Elizabeth got the impression that of all the posts he might have been assigned to, this had not been high on his list. "Besides, even if the squid were an intelligent species — and I'm considering that only as the kind of hypothetical question that entertains people with too much time on their hands — they only live in the water. They can't possibly care whether we salvage the ruins."

"Is that the case?" Teyla looked at two of the workers, who shuffled backwards, looking around as if unwilling to admit they'd spoken to her at all. "I understand you've had conflicts with the squid in the waters near the ruins. It is possible that you are disturbing their nesting grounds or areas that have ritual significance to them. It is also possible that they object to your presence here at all."

"I'm not interested in speculation. We've had problems with local animals. We're dealing with those problems. It's none of your concern."

"Its's our problem because we're trying to get these folks back where they want to be, and you're in our way," John said. "Otherwise, we'd be glad to go away and let you and the people here duke it out. But given that we're already involved, why don't we agree that we'll drop off Stripes' people —" Lynn cleared his throat audibly. "Once we've worked out a few things with the locals, and we won't interfere with your operations here?"

"That is a very nice promise," the Genii commander said. "And if it were just a matter of ferrying wildlife around for whatever ridiculous reasons your people have, we might be able to leave it at that. But now that we know that you have trained the creatures, we must obviously be on our guard against attempts to use them to spy on us."

"Oh, come on," John said. "We're not training them to spy on you."

"What is spying?" Stripes asked brightly.

"Sneaking around to see what others are doing," Elizabeth said.

"Oh! That is interesting to do!"

"And I'm sure you'll blame innocent animal curiosity when these things happen to swarm our divers and let you know if we make any finds that are worth coming back here to steal from under our noses," Minos said.

"I'm bringing the jumper in," John said. "We're not getting anywhere this way."

He brought it up to the beach and stepped out, followed by Lynn. Lynn looked at him questioningly, as if asking about something they'd talked about with the radio off, and John nodded.

"Our linguist here has an alternate request," he said. "We'll keep Stripes away from your work sites and won't bring any of the other squid through yet. In return, we'd like access to the ruins to look for inscriptions or writing that might provide some clues to the language of the creatures here. The local inhabitants must have lived with them for a long time after the Ancients left. If they were in contact with the creatures, there may be some records that would help us talk to them."

"It might even prove their intelligence to your satisfaction."

"You want to poke around in our salvage site," Minos said.

"We're not interested in technology or raw materials," Lynn said. "We don't even need to remove any artifacts, just take recordings."

"And if you stumble on Ancient technology, or a hoard of platinum bars? No, I don't think so."

"It would contribute to good relations between your people and our people," Elizabeth said.

"Do we have good relations?" Minos asked, raising an eyebrow.

Elizabeth met his gaze without backing down. She'd gotten the better of Genii with rifles while blindfolded and facing the threat of an imminent Wraith attack back home. She wasn't about to be intimidated by crankiness. "Don't you want to?"

After a moment he cursed under his breath, and she knew she'd won, at least for the moment. "You can stay," he said. "But you're not exploring on your own. I want you where I can keep an eye on you. Your linguist here —" He made the term sound like a dirty word. "He goes down with our divers. We review your recordings before you transmit them back to Atlantis. And anything he finds that's valuable, we keep."

"A real sweetheart of a deal," John said. "With generosity like that, it's no wonder the whole Pegasus Galaxy loves you."

"We didn't get where we are by being generous," Minos said. "Or by being trusting. Those are the terms. Take them or leave them."

John looked at Lynn, who nodded. "We'll take them," he said.

CHAPTER SIX

THE SUBMERSIBLE was cramped and smelled like the inside of a boot. William clambered in and plastered himself to the observation window, video camera in hand, while Sheppard peered in through the door. It looked anything but safe — the glass didn't seem thick enough, there was a good inch of water on the floor between the ribs and platforms William had crossed, and he wasn't sure he trusted the groaning air pumps, although having never spent time in a submarine back on Earth, for all he knew this was how they usually looked and sounded.

He glanced at Sheppard, who looked as skeptical as William felt. It was easy to get used to relying on Ancient technology, which, while prone to occasional catastrophic failure, or at least catastrophic failure to function as intended, usually worked seamlessly and gave the impression of being suitable for retail sale back on Earth. This was a reminder that most people's technology wasn't nearly as polished.

"I don't suppose you've ever been under the water in one of these," one of the crewmen said, a heavy-set man called Craden.

"I have been snorkeling a few times," William said.

"What is 'snorkeling'?"

"You put a plastic tube in your mouth, and then you kick your feet to move around under the surface of the water. It's recreational."

Craden snorted. "Recreational."

"Don't you guys do anything for fun but work and fight?" John asked.

"Back home, maybe. But we're not here for fun. We're here to get this job done so that we can get out of here. These are nasty waters. They look pretty, but nothing down there is friendly."

"Somebody stepped on a shiny shell and turned green and died," one of the other Genii said, and pantomimed choking and expiring.

"The seaweed gives you a rash. The crabs make you come out in blisters if they pinch you. And your friends the squid keep ramming everything in sight, from divers to the submersible to anything we're trying to haul out of the water. I swear this place is cursed," Craden said.

"Sounds like Australia," William said. "You can go, Colonel Sheppard. I'll be fine."

"Radio us if you have problems."

The door clanged shut behind him, and one of the Genii spun a wheel to lock it. There was a creaking, wheezing sound, and William couldn't help putting a hand to his throat.

"That's all the air being sucked out," Craden said. "If you black out, try not to fall face forward into the water."

"It's actually just the air being pumped out between the outer door and the inner one," one of the other crewmen offered. "Keeps the door shut."

"There's a safety tip," Craden said. "Don't open that door once we're underwater."

"I think I could have gotten that far," William said.

"I take it we're not going very far down."

"About thirty meters at the outside," Craden said. "We can go as deep as forty, but there's not much to find that far down. This used to be the point of an isthmus, so there's a narrow shelf where we're finding the ruins, and beyond that the sea floor drops off sharply. There's a large area of old buildings between here and the next island to the north, though, and that's what we're exploring right now."

He seemed to unbend a little while explaining his work, although the mood aboard the submersible was still not one of extreme good cheer.

"And what have you found so far?"

"A lot of things Minos would probably hang me up by my unmentionables for talking about," Craden said. "Generally speaking — metal. Plastic. A few devices, but nothing spectacular enough to get us rotated home and the heavy-hitting military scientists brought in."

"Inscriptions, art?"

"We've seen some walls with carvings. No lettering I recognize. Some metal plates with writing on them, too. Mostly they get hauled off to be melted down, if they're metal we can use."

"I don't suppose you have images or copies —"

"That's not what we're down here looking for. Personally, I'm not sure we're going to find anything as exciting as Minos is hoping for. The sea probably rose gradually, right? It's not like it could suddenly get deeper all over the planet."

"Unlikely, no," William said. "Melting polar ice caps could cause fairly rapid rise in sea level, but we're not talking about a catastrophic sudden immersion."

"So they would have hauled off everything portable and valuable they could carry. The only hope is that we'll find something really big and really valuable, and then how we're going to get it off this rock, I don't know."

"We're not," one of the other crewmen said. "If we find an Ancient installation or a sunken battlecruiser, they'll build a base here. And with our luck, we'll get posted here to do routine maintenance while we roast in the sun and rot from the damp."

"I think the inhabitants of this world might have something to say about that," William said.

"Yeah. Well. That would be a real shame, if you could prove that they don't want us here. It would make Minos look bad, all right. And we'd get reassigned. Possibly somewhere where there are bars to drink in and a climate that doesn't make you want to stay drunk all the time."

He didn't sound at all unhappy about the prospect. William hoped that would translate into patience with the pace of archaeological research, even the rushed version of it he planned to conduct.

"What's that?" he said, catching sight of something out the window. "That wall looks like it has some kind of inscription."

"All right," Craden said. He threw levers and spun a wheel, turning the submersible by slow degrees toward the stone wall. William peered out the window and began recording. To his pleasure, a section of the wall was inscribed in recognizable Ancient symbols; it was too much to hope for that he'd found a Rosetta stone right off the bat, but at least he could hope for some overlap between the Ancient inscription and the one in the local dialect. "Let's spend some time staring at a wall."

***

By mid-afternoon, Elizabeth was beginning to wish she'd brought a book to read. Although it was comfortable in the jumper, unlike outside where the tropical sun was making heat haze shimmer off the beach, she wasn't used to having nothing urgent to do. That was her problem in general, she suspected; she'd gotten used to being needed. There had been times when she'd been needed so much by the Atlantis mission that she'd wanted to point out sharply that there was only one of her, and she couldn't solve every problem for everyone.

Now, though, most of the time she could set her own priorities. There were plenty of useful things to research in the Pegasus Galaxy, but pure research had never been her primary interest. There were plenty of problems to solve, both in Atlantis and in Pegasus in general, but setting priorities for how to solve them wasn't up to her anymore. It was almost like being on vacation, after three years of intense struggle to keep her people alive.

She'd never done well with vacations. At least not unstructured ones. Simon had always told her that she didn't know how to relax, and that was probably true. But filling her calendar with museum visits and brisk walking tours wasn't really an option here. If she wanted to pick up the pace, she'd have to do that herself.

"Or I could just wait for the next life-threatening crisis," she said aloud. "That shouldn't take very long."

"Hoping for one?" John asked, raising an eyebrow.

"Maybe I'm just waiting for the other shoe to drop."

"I could run you and Teyla back to the gate," John offered.

"I'd rather be here in case we're needed," Elizabeth said. "I'm just not used to this much waiting without trying to answer a hundred emails and plan our next recreational volleyball tournament."

"I can totally hand that over to you."

"I wouldn't want to deprive you of the pleasure."

"We are getting a transmission from Dr. Lynn," Teyla said from the copilot's seat.

"So you've translated the squid's language already, right?" John said.

"Would that it were that simple. I've found some promising data that's allowed me to establish how the indigenous writing system matches Ancient phonemes, and I'm beginning to identify some patterns of linguistic drift. It would be nice if I could find anything that directly relates to the squid — right now I'm looking at public monuments and what I suspect may be advertising. But there are definitely some changes that are suggestive about potential drift in the language of the squid when you compare the data we collected back home with the data from the squid here."

John listened more patiently than Elizabeth expected. "What would help?"

"More observation of the squid. Can you take the jumper down and get some footage? Even a few more minutes of observing their interactions would help the computer establish more patterns that I can match up with what I'm seeing here."

"All right, but I'd better do it out of sight of the Genii up here, or they're going to get testy. Teyla, can you stay here and keep an eye on Minos? I think we're in a good place, but I don't want to miss it if he decides to call home and tell them that he's acquired some valuable hostages."

"Of course," she said. "Dr. Weir, will you stay as well? Minos seems to respect your status as the former leader of the Atlantis expedition. Perhaps that will keep him responsive."

"That would be nice," Elizabeth said. She climbed out of the jumper, pushing her hair out of her eyes and squinting in the bright sun. "Minos! Colonel Sheppard needs to go report back to Atlantis. We're going to stay here and wait for our linguist, if that's all right with you."

"If you stay out of the way of the work," Minos said. He wiped his forehead, and then gave Elizabeth a sidelong look. "So what did you do to wind up out of commission for so long?"

"I was injured in an attack on Atlantis," Elizabeth said. "Missing and presumed dead."

"So they always say. Crossed the wrong higher-ups, did you?"

"I wasn't in prison," Elizabeth said. "And certainly not imprisoned by my own people."

"But you're not in charge."

"Colonel Sheppard is doing an admirable job."

"And there's some question of your loyalty, after you

came back from wherever it was you were?"

"Certainly not," Elizabeth said. She hoped it sounded convincing, and was afraid it didn't. She'd always felt on firmer ground when she could tell at least part of the truth than when she had to lie.

"Politics," Minos said, and spat into the sand. "If there's anything worse, I don't know what it is."

***

"I think I'm getting somewhere," William said. He stretched cramped muscles, wishing for a workspace in which he could stand up without hitting his head on the ceiling or fit his knees entirely under the console in front of him. His latest computer model was producing some intelligible speech that he hoped wasn't completely unrelated to the patterns being displayed by the indigenous squid. "Those inscriptions went a long way toward providing what I needed. If I can get even a few more samples to work with —"

"We're running out of down time," one of the Genii said.

"Yes, we are," Craden said. "You're going to have to work with what you've got. Our air supply isn't unlimited."

"Well, I must admit I'm in favor of having air. Once we surface, I can get a second opinion from Stripes."

"He's really intelligent?" Craden asked skeptically.

"Yes, certainly. I wouldn't think that would be so strange to you, having known all your life that there was alien intelligent life in your galaxy. It was a definite shock when I found out there was alien intelligent life in mine."

"Wraith are one thing," Craden said. "Talking fish is another thing. It's a little too much like something out of a children's story, not that our children's stories usually talk about tentacles that drag you down into the dark, stinking…"

Something jolted the hull. "Will you watch where you're going?" Craden snapped at the navigator. "Whatever you've found, it's not interesting enough to want to crash into it."

"We didn't hit something," the navigator said. "I think something hit us."

Immense arms slid across the glass of the submersible's window, suckers the size of William's fist flexing and deforming as they skidded across the surface. One tentacle batted at the window, smaller, hook-like protrusions scraping at it.

The glass is strong, William told himself. It must be, or it couldn't hold back the pressure of the water or deal with running into even small pieces of debris. A tentacle isn't going to break it.

There was another, heavier thud as something hard slammed into the glass. William registered that it was the beak of another giant squid as the creature turned and buffeted the glass with the length of its body, its great dark eye fixing on William for an eternal-seeming moment before it slid past.

"Damn it, they're ramming us," Craden said. "Get us out of here."

"We can take it though, right?" William said.

"You should hope. Reverse engines, back us away from these things."

The squid were flashing angry patterns, and William remembered the tablet in his lap. He turned back to it, hoping that the jumper's computer had processed enough data to get some kind of intelligible speech out of it. "We… you… above… cold! A feeling!"

That last, William was fervently sure, was "anger." He added that bit of data and spared a glance for the furious motion around him in the submersible.

The navigator was backing the craft away from the squid. Craden was biting his lip, but looked reassured with every decimeter they put between themselves and the pursuing tentacles. As soon as they were clear, they could surface, and then even if the glass broke, they'd be in better shape, although the vision of breaking glass and probing tentacles attempting to rip the intruders out of the control room wasn't a pleasant one even if he imagined being able to breathe in the process.

There was a leaden thud, and the submersible stopped moving. Then it jolted violently, and William was thrown back against the bulkhead, only the cramped space he'd wedged himself into preventing him from going flying into one of the Genii or measuring his length on the sodden floor. He cringed at the sound of metal being strained and wrenched, and Craden swore at an even worse sound: the quiet of the engines going dead. From the jolting of the submersible and its sudden sideways drift, William suspected they had been wrenched free of the craft, or at least operative pieces of them had been.

The sound of the air pump continued, a small mercy, and then slowed to a clunking stop the moment William had begun to be relieved. Of course, it was being operated by the engines. Battery backup power wasn't an option here. His alarm deepened as the submersible began to pitch and slew sideways.

"Keep on the rudders," Craden said. "You can hold us steady even if we can't move. And radio Minos. He can get a boat out, but we've got to get to the surface for them to pick us up."

"If we can't move, isn't that going to be a problem? Especially in a small container with limited air?" William asked pointedly.

"What, you like to breathe?" Craden snorted, black humor seeming to steady him. "We can jettison ballast to surface even if we don't have propulsion. Start jettisoning ballast," he ordered, and there was a series of jolting clanks as several somethings were levered free of the submersible's outer hull by nakedly geared machinery.

All right, William told himself. The laws of physics still applied. They might not be able to go sideways, but given enough buoyancy, they could definitely go up. And the air in the submersible ought to make it buoyant enough to rise.

For a moment, it did, and William craned his neck to look out the window, hoping for the sight of the submersible breaking the waves. Instead, he saw tentacles — significantly more tentacles — and felt a heavy jolt as the submersible's ascent stopped.

"What's happening?"

"Maybe one of them's caught on our hull somewhere," one of the Genii suggested.

Craden shook his head. "One wouldn't stop us from surfacing."

"I don't believe it's one," William said. He nodded out the window. Several of the creatures were visible, wrapping their tentacles around every convenient protrusion and pulling the submersible down. "I think they're working together."

There was an even heavier jolt that went through the soles of William's feet, and the submersible pitched sideways. William tried to tuck himself into a ball, and then his head struck something painfully, and the world reeled for an indeterminate amount of time. He wound up lying on his back on what he identified after a moment as the bulkhead, water soaking through his clothes.

Water. That was a bad sign. He struggled up to his elbows, feeling for his radio, which wasn't where he expected it to be. Probably jarred loose by the same impact that was making his head throb. "Are we taking on water?"

"Doesn't look like it," Craden said. It was dim, only a little light filtering through the window, which he registered was half-buried in the sand of the ocean floor. "Could be a slow leak, but we'd run out of air before we had to worry about it."

"We could swim for the surface," William proposed experimentally, although he had never been a champion swimmer. He felt that the threat of drowning would be quite motivational. "And then call for the jumper to come and pick us up."

"Would you care to take your chances out there with

those things?" Craden said. William contemplated the nearest saucer-sized eye. It was probably his imagination that it looked visibly angry — it wasn't as if the squid had any human facial features to produce expressions with — but it certainly wasn't something he cared to view at close range while possibly being grasped by tentacles or bitten by the forearm-length beaks of the creatures outside.

"Plan B, then," William said, as his hand finally closed on the radio. "I'll radio the jumper and they can come down here and..." He trailed off. The jumper's shields could normally envelop another vehicle, allowing them to simply walk to the jumper in safety. That was how Sheppard and Radek had rescued Rodney from a jumper in much deeper water before William had joined the expedition. But if they couldn't use the shields, their options were much more limited.

"Shoot these things? I like that idea. You've got those drone things, don't you? All we've got is sidearms, and they're not going to do us any good underwater even if we could open the hatch to take a shot."

"I suppose spear guns aren't in your usual military gear?"

"No, because we're not usually in pits like this," Craden muttered as William activated his radio.

"Colonel Sheppard? We have a problem."

CHAPTER SEVEN

ELIZABETH BROKE off her conversation with Minos as her radio crackled and a larger, bulkier radio unit at his belt sounded an alarmed squeal. He looked at her suspiciously and turned to answer the call.

"What's going on?" Elizabeth said into her radio.

"Lynn and the Genii team are pinned down by the local squid," John said. "I've got eyes on them, but my options are limited."

"Can you repair the engines?" Minos was asking. "What do you mean, 'torn off'?"

"Do you want me to tell Minos you're on the scene?"

"Might as well," John said. "His people are in this mess too."

"Captain Minos," Elizabeth said. "Colonel Sheppard has your submersible in view from our jumper."

"Let me talk to him," Minos said. "Sheppard! Get those creatures away from our ship!"

"Now you need our help?"

Minos's face turned even redder. "We would appreciate your help," he said through gritted teeth. "And your man is trapped down there as well. Our submersible doesn't mount any weapons. I know that your jumpers do, so fire away."

"Wait," Elizabeth said immediately.

"In your own time, but you should know our submersible has a limited supply of air. If you'd like your man to continue breathing, I suggest you find a way to extract him — and our crew — before the air runs out or one of those creatures punches a hole in the side and starts eating them."

"We don't have a lot of options here," John said. "Dr. Lynn, how are you doing down there?"

"We've been better," Lynn said. "But I got the data you sent, and I think there may be a chance — I'm sending my analysis over to the jumper right now —"

"I mean how are you doing given that you're being attacked by giant squid?"

"Ah. Well. Please do feed the data that I'm giving you into the jumper's computers. It's a little tricky to run analyses right now because the submersible is on its side, and we're beginning to take on a significant amount of water. Also, there are several creatures wrapped around the submersible, and from the — er — muscular contractions of the tentacles I'm looking at, it appears to me that they're trying to squeeze us in a coordinated effort designed to crack the submersible open like an egg. At which point we will certainly have severe difficulties. But, Colonel Sheppard, my data —"

"You may not care if those things eat your people, but I'm not about to watch them eat mine," Minos said. "Shoot them now."

"Wait," Elizabeth said. "We may still have other options —"

"We're out of options."

"Don't do it, Colonel," Elizabeth said.

"The problem is that he's right," John said. "A couple of drone launches nearby should make it clear to the squid what they're dealing with, and maybe they'll scatter."

"Do not shoot."

"You are not in a position to give that order," John said. "In case you've forgotten."

Elizabeth gritted her teeth. "I haven't forgotten," she said. "This is a request. Please. Don't fire on those people."

"We are out of other choices."

"No, we're not. Try talking to them using the data that Dr. Lynn just sent over. He's willing to take the risk."

"I'm not," John said.

"Neither am I," Minos said. He grabbed her in one quick motion and pulled her back against his chest, the cool metal of a sidearm pressing against temple. "I've had enough of standing around while my people are being attacked by a monster. Shoot them, or I shoot Dr. Weir."

"This is a mistake," Teyla said.

"We don't negotiate with kidnappers," John said.

"Now that would be a mistake. I'm not bluffing," Minos said. Elizabeth could smell his sweat and feel the metal of the barrel digging into her skin.

"Yes, you are," she said calmly. "If you shoot me, Colonel Sheppard will have no remaining motivation to rescue your people. Even if he does attack the squid and get Dr. Lynn out of there, he can simply leave your people to drown."

"He wouldn't," Minos said.

"Do you really want to bet?"

"You are making an unwise choice," Teyla said to

Minos, looking as if she were judging whether she could safely disarm him. She met Elizabeth's eyes in a wordless question, and Elizabeth shook her head the slightest fraction. She'd rather play this scene out. Teyla relaxed slightly, but remained poised for action. "I hope you will not have occasion to learn quite how unwise."

"Colonel Sheppard," Elizabeth continued. "Let me try to negotiate a peaceful solution."

He sounded as if he were gritting his teeth. "With a gun to your head?"

"Yes. With a gun to my head. I've done it before. It's why I'm here."

"You can give it one try," he said. "I'm patching you through."

***

John patched Elizabeth's transmission through the jumper's translation program and then sat with his hands poised above the control panel, watching the knot of arms and tentacles tighten around the submersible. He wouldn't even have to hit a button to shoot. All it would take was a thought. He held back the jumper from launching the drones, although every instinct cried out to fire.

"We mean you no harm," Elizabeth said. "We come here from another world bringing your kin." John waited, hoping the translation would work.

"That is strange talking!" Stripes said, rushing out in front of John's jumper. "I do not understand it!"

"Stripes, get back, it's not safe," John said. He'd seen enthusiastic kids put themselves in the middle of danger zones before. It hadn't ever ended well.

"What are they doing? They will break your ship! You are air-breathers!"

"Get out from in front of the jumper."

"The squid who tried to speak with you earlier is Stripes," Elizabeth said. John could see from the light that filtered through the water that the jumper's shield was changing colors, but he wasn't sure how much the creatures were taking it in. "He is one of your own descendants. The beings in the ship — the metal object — that you are attacking right now are intelligent. You will hurt them if you continue. Please stop."

"Saying please isn't going to help," Minos snapped over the radio.

"You know, I find that it rarely hurts," Elizabeth said.

The tentacles tightened on the submersible, and there was a rush of air bubbles from a pipe that had snapped free. John tensed. It would only take a single thought to launch the drones, and hesitating could be the worst decision he'd ever made.

Then one of the squid unwound itself from around the submersible and arrowed directly for him. He stood his ground, trusting that he'd be able to veer off at least enough to blunt its attack if it intended to ram him.

Instead it took up a posture that appeared angry, but wasn't an immediate attack. "You, the air-breathers, brought. You brought the air-breathers here," the computer translated, apparently grasping the syntax at last.

"We did not bring the other humans here," Elizabeth said. "They are from a different world, and they came here on their own."

"This one. The strange one who looks like us but does

not speak like us. He brought the other humans here. He allowed them to disturb the places where we teach our young. It is forbidden for strangers to go there. That is the sheltered place, where the small grow to become large before they enter the open ocean."

"It makes sense," John said. "There are probably predators here, not like back where we came from. They'd have to be more protective of their kids."

"I only brought humans here today!" Stripes said. "I have never been here before!"

"We came here with one of your descendants today," Elizabeth said. "The other humans must have been here for weeks or months. We are not responsible for their coming, but some of their people are trapped in the submersible — the metal object — along with one of our people. They need to return to the surface so that they can breathe. Please release them."

"They should not have come," the squid said.

"We can discuss conditions for their staying or leaving."

"Now wait a minute," Minos demanded. "I never said we were interested in discussing conditions."

"And I'm cutting the transmission to the squid," John said. "Minos, if you're not willing to negotiate for your people's return, we might as well grab our man and go home. You can figure out how to get the squid to let yours go without even listening to what they want."

"I won't forget this, Lantean."

"Yeah, your people never do," John said. "Opening up the transmission again."

"Before we discuss conditions, please release the

humans, or at least lift their metal device to the surface so that they can have air to breathe while we talk," Elizabeth said. "We are armed with weapons that can kill, and if our people die, we will have little remaining reason not to use them. But we would rather negotiate than fight."

There was a nerve-wracking pause, and then the squid wrapped around the submersible released their grip on it. From its rapid upward ascent like a bobbing cork, John gathered that it had already jettisoned enough ballast that it floated now that the squid weren't pulling it down. He surfaced as well, and was relieved to see the craft opening a small hatch to vent its air, although several squid swam defensive circles around it, barring his way if he had any idea of rescuing its inhabitants.

"We do not want these air-breathers to live in our oceans," the squid said. "They disturb our young in the cliffs under the sea and eat our fish. There is only enough here for us."

"They have no intention of living here permanently," Elizabeth said. "They come only to take metal and other things created by the humans who once lived here out of the water."

"Humans," the creature said. It spoke with others in the water surrounding it, a murmur of voices that corresponded to a rapid series of clashing and discordant patterns. "Air-breathers. We have stories of those. Living on the land. They spoke to us. Strange words. Strange air-breathers."

"Yes. The cities, these buildings — the stone and metal

cliffs near the shore — they were built by humans, long ago. They left behind things that the Genii are hunting for. Metals, and anything that might have been part of an Ancient device — crystals that glow, or that don't seem natural. Once they have found them, they will go."

"Believe me, I'd like nothing more," Minos muttered over the radio.

"Metal things. We have seen metal things, under the sea. And crystal things, that glow. Some are here in the cliffs where we teach the young, on this side of the island. We do not want you here, among our people and our young. But there is other metal in places where we hunt, sometimes." The squid broke off again. More muttering, more flashing colors. "If you take the metal from those places, will you leave the cliffs here alone? If you have the metal, will you go?"

"Can they help us find the metal?" Minos said.

"Now you want their help?" John said, rolling his eyes. "If it'll help us find what we're looking for faster, sure."

"We can show you," the squid said. "We have no use for metal. And we want you to go soon."

"I think we can work something out," Minos said.

"That leaves the second question." Elizabeth's voice was calm, and whatever was going on back on the surface, he trusted that she could handle the situation with Minos. That didn't make him like the situation any better. "Stripes and some of his friends from our planet would like to return here, to live among you. They were taken through the Stargate — through a passageway that leads from one world to another — a long time ago. Some of those who left your world back then are still alive. They would very much like to come home."

"We do not remember this," the squid said cautiously.

"It was long ago," Elizabeth said. "Many thousands of years."

"Then how can some still live?"

"Those of your people who went to the other world were changed by their experiences," Elizabeth said. "They became extremely long-lived. I believe they are much like you, but that will be a difference between you. They will live for many centuries, while generations of your people come and go. If your people and theirs mate, I'm not sure —"

"We would not mate with strangers," the creature said, knotting its tentacles in what looked to John like an unhappy posture.

"I'm sure I'm in no position to predict that. I'm only saying that I honestly don't know what combining their genes and yours would do. It might give their descendants here the same long life, or it might not. They will have to think about that seriously, as will you. But they are your long-lost kin, however different they may now seem. And while I can't say what effects their genetic diversity might have on your people, I am certain of one thing — there are many things you can learn from them, and many things they can learn from you. Here in the Pegasus Galaxy — in this sea of stars — our own people have met our long-lost kin, and we are profoundly richer for the experience."

There was a lengthy pause. Minos made a noise that sounded suspiciously like a snort, but said nothing. The squid floated in the water outside the window, subtle shades rippling across their skin.

"We have conditions," the squid said.

John could imagine Elizabeth's expression without her having to say a word, that fierce, satisfied look she got when she'd managed to broker a deal.

"Of course," Elizabeth said. "What did you have in mind?"

"Only small numbers may come at first," the squid said. "We will swim with them, and learn about these beings who you say are our long-lost kin. We will teach them our language, and hear what they have made of themselves on this far-off world. We will see what it is like to have people who do not age among us. If they do not cause harm here, then we will allow more to come."

"That suits us fine, and I think it will suit them as well," Elizabeth said. "We can only bring one or two individuals here at a time in our ships. It will be some time before any large numbers could possibly come here."

"What about the rest of your species?" John asked, breaking in. "Will they agree that you have the right to make this decision?"

"Some will not," the squid said. "But those of us who live and teach our young here near the sunken cliffs will accept my decision. Or they will go elsewhere, and trouble those who remain here no more. And others have no right to come here, so we do not care what they think about who we allow to live here. It is none of their business."

It wasn't great, but John wasn't particularly optimistic about the idea of getting an entire planet full of squid to agree to anything. It's not as if Earth were particularly good at that, either. At the end of the day, it generally boiled down to what the people in control of the Stargate decided to do, and that wasn't any different here than anywhere else.

"Good enough," John said. "Now, if you'll move away from our ship, we can retrieve our people." The ring of circling squid parted, and John brought the jumper to the surface to hover just above the waves. He opened the back cargo hatch as the submersible pitched and rolled. "Dr. Lynn, can you get everybody up to an exit that's not underwater?"

"I think so," William said. A hatch on the submersible opened, and William scrambled up, slipping and stumbling on the submersible's surface but managing to catch at the back cargo hatchway of the jumper and haul himself inside. John was unfastening safety webbing, and he tossed it out for the Genii crew to hang onto and clamber aboard.

"Can you tow her?" Craden asked.

"If we take it slowly. Show me where I can grapple her onto my ship without ripping pieces off, and we'll see if we can get your ship to land."

The jumpers weren't designed to act as tugboats, but John managed to haul the jury-rigged submarine up the beach until it grounded itself on the sand. Craden and the other Genii climbed out of the jumper the moment John opened the door. John uncoupled the Genii submersible and then frowned at the readings he was picking up. Another Genii boat had approached, and it was dropping something over the side that had a troubling energy signature.

"What's going on?" he asked Elizabeth over the radio.

"I'm fine, but something's off here," Elizabeth said. "Stay in the jumper until I get a better read on what's going on."

***

"Right," Minos was saying over his radio. "The structures on the south side of the island." He had finally released Elizabeth, although one of the other Genii was still pointing a rifle at her. She hadn't thought he had any intention of really shooting her. From what she'd seen of Minos, he was the kind of person who wanted an easy way out of his difficulties, and was just smart enough to understand that killing a member of the Atlantis expedition wouldn't really smooth his path for him.

Out to sea, Elizabeth could see a sturdy workhorse of a boat approaching, its deck piled high with equipment. As she watched, the Genii on its deck heaved something over the side, then moved some distance toward the island and heaved a second piece of machinery over.

"That looks like precisely where the squid said they didn't want you diving," she said.

"We're not planning on diving," Minos said. "And it's time for you and your people to leave."

"I take it I'm no longer a hostage," Elizabeth said tartly, and one of the Genii lowered the weapon that was pointed at her.

"I've just watched them dropping multiple objects with energy signatures," John said into her earpiece. "I don't think they're nice gifts for their hosts, here.

What's your present situation? I can come and get you—"

The radio crackled, and when Minos didn't pick it up, Elizabeth reached out and activated it before Minos could stop her. "We've got three of the explosives in place," a man's voice said. "We'll drop the others where we're seeing the most activity from the creatures."

"Copy that," Minos said, meeting Elizabeth's eyes without shame, and switched the radio off.

Elizabeth shook her head in disbelief. "I thought we had a deal." It shouldn't surprise her that the Genii were still looking for a military solution, but it did surprise her that they were willing to break their agreement so flagrantly.

"You wanted to prove that we were dealing with an intelligent species here," Minos said. "You did. Which means that we've got to send a message strong enough to keep them away from these islands and away from our work. Seeing as they're intelligent, they'll learn quickly enough that we've got weapons that can destroy their nurseries. And then we'll finally be able to carry out our operation in peace."

"So you're simply going to drop explosives," Elizabeth said.

"Copy that," John said in her ear. "I'm going after them." Elizabeth bit back any reply she might have made, not wanting to provide any warning of John's intentions. She hoped that the Genii underestimated the capabilities of the jumper, and also hoped that John wasn't overestimating them given the jumper's current lack of shields.

"The indigenous inhabitants of this planet can help

you," Teyla said. "You do not have to do this."

"Suppose that's actually true," Minos said, looking weary. "Do you think that if I go home and tell my superiors that I'm working with a bunch of squid that I'll get a commendation for that? 'Don't worry, the squid say they'll help us find the best artifacts and carry them off. They wouldn't possibly hold the best things back for themselves.' I'll be a laughing-stock, and then I'll get told to handle the squid problem and take it all."

"These are the remains of an entire civilization," Elizabeth said. "You can't take it all." If nothing else, keeping Minos talking was giving John time to act. "And the squid aren't using these things. They don't have any reason to lie to you."

"I can take everything that's worth anything, and leave the rest for your tentacled friends. But if I'm ever going to get off this rotten excuse for a planet, I can't do that by cozying up to a bunch of invertebrates."

"Radim is a reasonable leader. I'm sure he would prefer for you to find a solution that's effective even if it isn't the bloodiest and most hard-headed solution available," Elizabeth said, beginning to lose her patience.

"Where's Sheppard?" Minos said abruptly. "I'm not interested in disposing of an unwanted past commanding officer for him, if that's what Sheppard has in mind." One of his men brought up his rifle to target her again, but Minos looked on edge, trying to balance too many factors. She didn't believe he'd shoot until he understood what was going on.

"He doesn't think there's any point in talking to you

right now," Elizabeth said. "I expect he's gone back to the gate to report."

"Without you."

"I still think there's a point in talking."

"Talk all you want," Minos said. "We'll be taking action."

CHAPTER EIGHT

SHEPPARD SPED the jumper through the water, racing after the first of the explosives. Around it, colorful clouds of fish sped like flocks of brilliant parrots, veering away from the jumper at the last minute. William watched the sleeker shapes that circled further away, probably the watchful squid. They observed but didn't interfere as the jumper approached a large, regularly-shaped metal object that had come to rest among the crumbled remains of a concrete wall.

"Is that the explosive device?" William asked.

"Yep."

"How are we going to disarm it?"

"I'll think of something."

"When?" William asked after a moment's pause.

"Don't be a smartass unless you have a plan. If I shoot it with a drone, I'll do more damage than if I just let it explode. If I had diving gear, I could go out there and try to disarm it by hand. Even without diving gear, I could go out and try to disarm it by hand, except that without the shields I don't have any way of getting out of the jumper without it filling up with water."

"A problem," William said. He didn't point out that it was also a problem that they were sitting a few meters away from an explosive device in a ship with no shields. That seemed to go without saying.

Several small squid, smaller than Stripes, appeared

and began swimming curiously toward the explosive device. One of them extended tentacles toward it, their tips tinted a faint pink like flower petals.

"Those are children," William said, his stomach dropping, and turned the communications system back on. "Move away, please! This is very dangerous! Do not touch the metal thing!"

The small squid turned to look the jumper with the same curiosity. Several of them swam in excited circles back and forth between the jumper and the explosive. William could almost believe they were daring one another to touch it.

"Hey, Stripes!" John said.

"I am here!" the squid said, swimming into view.

"Get those kids away from that device," he said. "It may explode — make lots of sharp things that fly apart very fast and hurt anyone they hit. It's not safe for them to come near it."

Stripes rushed toward the group of squid, turning a series of lurid colors and patterns that the computer rendered only as a wordless yell. The small squid scattered, apparently finding an inarticulately yelling stranger alarming when a strange device and a talking ship weren't. They retreated, although not far enough for William's comfort, and he could see unblinking eyes and tentacle tips peeking out from behind seaweed-covered stone.

"We're going to have to grapple and tow it," John said. "If I can hook onto it with the gear we were using to tow the submersible, we may be in business." He maneuvered the jumper cautiously, backing it up toward the explosive in an attempt to snag it.

"And this won't make it explode," William said, trying not to make it a question.

"If it were designed to detonate on contact, it would have exploded when it hit the bottom. It's either on a timer, or the Genii are waiting to detonate them all at once. Which makes the most tactical sense, in an evil kind of way, because otherwise, the first explosion is going to scatter the squid and reduce the amount of damage they can do."

"So, no, right?"

"Now you sound like McKay," Sheppard said. There was a thump, and he let out an unsatisfied breath. "I haven't got it."

"Stripes!" William said. "Can you hook the grapple onto the mine?"

"I don't know those words!"

"The metal thing coming off of our ship. Can you put it onto that metal thing out there, the round bumpy one, so that we can move it?"

"Yes!" the squid said cheerfully, and a moment later, William felt the jumper jerk and move more heavily through the water.

"Great," John said. "We're going to take this one out to sea, and then come back for the next one. You'll help, right?"

"Of course!"

"If we run out of time…" William said.

"Then we'll all have problems together," Sheppard replied.

***

"You made a deal," Elizabeth said. "Whether your superiors will like it or not, you made a bargain. If you don't keep it, that weakens the ability of anyone else in the Pegasus Galaxy to trust that the Genii will keep their word."

"You already don't trust us," Minos said.

"It's not just about the Atlantis mission. Word does get around."

"That we cleaned out some squid!"

"That you made a bargain with the inhabitants of one of the planets you claim, and then broke your word," Teyla said. "If we cannot honor our agreements with one another, we will have war among the humans of this galaxy, and that will not be good for anyone."

"We didn't make an agreement with other humans," Minos said. "We told these creatures what they wanted to hear while we were making arrangements to protect our interests. Human interests."

"So these people aren't human enough for you to feel that their lives have value," Elizabeth said. "That's interesting for you to say. It seems to me that's the justification that the Wraith used for refusing to negotiate with humans in the past."

"The Wraith eat us," Minos said.

"Which is precisely why they couldn't afford to recognize us as fellow sentient beings before they had another choice, because it was too difficult for them to reconcile their need to feed on us with acknowledging that we were also people. But these creatures are not your only source of food. Killing them isn't necessary for you and your people to survive. It's just a convenient way for you to advance your career. I think the Wraith have the moral high ground there."

"I have no choice."

"That's not true. You can choose to keep your word. And by doing so, you can protect your government's reputation and the alliances between humans in this galaxy. I don't know whether your commanding officer will appreciate that or not. But if they don't, they should."

***

"How many of these things did they drop?" William asked. John checked the control panel again. "Five," he said. "We've got three."

"How much time —"

"Not a good question to ask," John said. "But the last two are close together."

They raced toward them through the water. John would have given a lot to be navigating the jumper through air or vacuum rather than the water that dragged at their hull and slowed them down, but the last two mines were in sight. He could see more of the small squid investigating the metal objects, drawn to them with the familiar awful curiosity of civilians and children everywhere.

Several larger squid appeared in front of the jumper, suddenly enough that John had to draw it up abruptly to avoid plowing into them. They flashed a series of angry-looking patterns, and William activated the translation program again.

"Move away, strange creatures," one of the squid said. Their voices were monotones, the translation program clearly not reliably recognizing the equivalent of intonation, but John felt that he could put the music to the words.

"You should not be here," another said.

"Move away from our young."

"Strange creatures."

"Wrong creatures."

"We're trying to help," John said, gritting his teeth. "See those metal things that the boat dropped? They're explosives. They're going to fly apart and hurt anyone who's close to them." The squid were circling around the jumper now, effectively blocking his progress.

He weighed the damage he would cause by barreling through them against the catastrophe of the explosives detonating. However that math came out, he wasn't sure how much damage they would cause to the jumper in the process.

As if in answer to his thought, the jumper jerked, and he realized that one — or more — of the creatures had grasped the grappling gear.

"Let go!" Stripes said. "We need that!"

"They can't understand you," William said, although from the jerking of the jumper, there was a scuffle outside that probably required no translation.

"Don't fight with them, just —" John began, and then broke off as the jumper suddenly lurched forward, no longer weighted down by the grasp of tentacles.

"Was that —" William asked.

John clenched his fists. "We just lost the grapples."

"Stripes, can you move the explosive — the metal things — by yourself?" William asked.

"I think so! But they will not let me through!" Stripes darted back and forth, attempting to find a way through the protectively screening squid, but they guarded the area containing the explosives, not letting Stripes find an opening. The charges had come to rest in what looked like the remains of a courtyard, and John could see small squid, some only the length of his arm, swimming in and out of the doorways and gaping windows.

"We've got to get the charges even if we have to go through some people to do it. Hold onto the jumper," John said to Stripes. "I'll get you close, and you grab hold. Try to get them both if you can."

"I will try!"

He sent the jumper forward, wincing at the thumps as he hit the squid in front of him. The jumper jerked under the weight of tentacles, and the forward viewscreen was occluded by suckers and enormous eyes. John kept the jumper moving forward and tried not to think about monster movies. The kraken, splitting ships in half — radioactive monsters in B movies, pulling toy ships underwater against a badly painted background —

"I can reach them!" Stripes exclaimed. He held the jumper in place, hovering above the explosives, Stripes clinging to the bottom of the jumper tenaciously. Something dark was spreading in the water.

"You okay?" he asked.

"I am all right," Stripes said, although he sounded less enthusiastic than usual. "I have the two devices! I am holding tight to them and to your ship!"

"Fasten your seatbelt," John said, and sent the jumper rising straight up as fast as he could go.

As he had hoped, it was the direction the squid had least expected. He felt the drag on the ship loosen, and two of the creatures that were splayed across the window slid away, suckers and heavy arms thumping as they went.

"It is hard to hold on!" Stripes said.

John brought the jumper around in a tight circle. "We're not going far."

"This isn't the way out to deeper water," William pointed out.

"You got it. Stripes, you can drop the devices right here."

"I am dropping them!" the squid said. The explosives came to rest in the shallows, right where John wanted them, nestled between the hull of the docked Genii boat and the beached submersible.

"Good job," John said, and patched his radio signal through to Elizabeth. "Dr. Weir? I've got some information that Minos might want to know."

***

"You have a lot of faith in the altruism of my superiors," Minos said.

Elizabeth paused as John spoke. "I wouldn't say that," she temporized.

"We've put the last two charges right next to the Genii craft," John said over the radio. "If they explode, they'll take out their own ships. I'm going to let you decide how to play this, but find out if the devices are on a timer. If they are, you'd better warn him now."

"That sounds like what you're saying to me," Minos said.

Elizabeth returned her attention to Minos. "You're not going to detonate those while we're still talking, are you?"

"I'm listening," Minos said. "And holding off on detonating. Yet."

"I'm glad to hear that you're not detonating them yet," Elizabeth said for John's benefit. "And I think you'll be glad that you listened. For the record I'm not placing any faith in the altruism of your superiors, only in their practicality. The creatures near this island are only a small part of the population of this planet. It's possible that you might have been able to eradicate a hostile unintelligent species, but now you know that's not what you're dealing with. I think that you'll find it incredibly difficult to conduct an effective mining operation with a war going on."

"She has a point," Craden said unexpectedly. "We've had the worst time trying to work with those things ramming our ships and going after our divers. If we give them reason to go after us, it's only going to get worse, not better."

"Not if they're successfully scared off," Minos muttered. Craden and the rest of the crew of the submersible didn't look persuaded, though, and Elizabeth pressed her argument.

"In my experience, Captain — and I assure you, I have considerable experience with people who've thought the same way on Earth — attacking people's homes and families rarely scares them off. It only makes them determined to exact revenge. And being the target of that revenge is hardly going to speed up your mining operations here. I'm not saying you shouldn't defend yourselves, if attacked. But give the bargain you've struck a chance."

"If, as you say, what you want is a successful mission, I believe this is your best hope of that success," Teyla said. "It may be your fastest way home."

Minos let out a frustrated breath. "I'm not saying my government recognizes those sea monsters as inhabitants with rights to this planet," he said. "In fact, I plan on saying as little as possible to my government about this entire series of events. But, all right. I'll try it your way."

"I think you won't be sorry," Elizabeth said. "Especially since at the moment, detonating your explosives would blow up your own submersible and salvage vessel." She nodded toward the harbor, and Minos narrowed his eyes and jerked his chin toward one of his men, who splashed out knee-deep into the water, and then hastily retreated up the beach.

Minos let out a long, slow breath. "And exactly why aren't you in charge of the Atlantis mission again?"

"As you suspected," Elizabeth said dryly. "They don't entirely trust me."

"I can see why."

"Since at this point I think we trust each other approximately the same amount, it's a fortunate coincidence that we'll be making repeated trips here with Stripes' people," she said. "That will give us the opportunity to appreciate your successful salvage mission, which we wouldn't dream of interfering with, although of course if some kind of conflict had broken out between the Genii and the local inhabitants, we'd have to take that situation as it comes."

"I'm sure we'll be thrilled to see you," Minos said, and spat into the sand.

***

It took some persuading for John to get Stripes loaded back into the jumper; he was determined to explore their new world. Teyla was the one who finally persuaded him that it was his duty to return and tell his people what he had seen.

"I promise, you'll be one of the first we transport back here," Elizabeth said.

"That is not very likely," Stripes said, his arms and tentacles drooping. "There are many older than me who are more important."

"I think what you have learned will make you an important person as well," Teyla said, and he made what John was beginning to recognize as happy circles around the cramped jumper cargo compartment, plastering one eye to the partition again as the jumper lifted out of the water.

Elizabeth settled into the co-pilot's seat as John turned back toward the Stargate. There was a silence. John wasn't sure whether it was an awkward silence or not.

"I didn't want to call you down like that back there," he said.

"You're in charge, and sometimes you have to make that clear," Elizabeth said. "Believe me, I understand that. For what it's worth, I wasn't trying to challenge your authority."

"For what it's worth, I'd turn command over to you in a heartbeat if that's the way the IOA calls it," John said. "If things had gone differently — if we'd dealt with the Replicators better — maybe you wouldn't ever have lost it in the first place."

"I don't blame you for my... I suppose I should call it death, although that seems metaphysically complicated. Or for anything that happened afterwards. You did everything you could to save me, and in the end, I found my way home."

"Which is a good thing," John said. It seemed inadequate, but the look in her eyes said it wasn't.

"And I don't blame you for being in charge now. I won't say it's never frustrating. There are times when I'd make a different call, and I wish I still had the authority to play it my way. But I don't resent you for it. If anything, I'm proud to be able to say that I had some role in making you the leader that you are today."

He cleared his throat, managing a casual drawl. "So, does that mean that you're going to follow my orders without arguing from now on?"

Elizabeth smiled. "Exactly as much as you always followed mine," she said, and leaned back in her seat to watch the Stargate appearing on the horizon.

Stay in touch...
Follow us on Twitter
@StargateNovels

Find us on Facebook at
facebook.com/StargateNovels

Sign up for our newsletter
at StargateNovels.com

THANKS!

STARGATE SG·1.   STARGATE ATLANTIS

Original novels based on the hit
TV shows **STARGATE SG-1** and
STARGATE ATLANTIS

Available as e-books from leading online
retailers

Paperback editions available from
Amazon and IngramSpark

If you liked this book, please tell your
friends and leave a review on a
bookstore website. Thanks!

Made in the USA
Monee, IL
24 February 2022

91755822R00073